A Most
Useful Betrothal

A Most Useful Betrothal

NETTA FEI

VIDE INC

ISBN: 979-8-9901381-1-7 - Paperback
eISBN: 979-8-9901381-0-0 - eBook

∞This paper meets the requirements of ANSI/NISO Z39.48-1992 (Permanence of Paper)

072524

To Poppie and Jaack, the origins of my universe.

CHAPTER 1

BECOMING

*[be- 'kom-ING]: the process of coming
to be something or of passing into a state.*

I BECOME TWO-THIRDS MARRIED TODAY. At fifteen years old, it's coming later than when most Ebre Y'israelite virgins wed. It wasn't a desire of mine until my heart, enraged by the horrors of social caste, compelled me to give a suitor my consent—the first of the three legal requirements for a marriage to be valid. The second one is arriving any moment now.

Inside the main entrance of Ramah, where I live, council elders sit on benches to my left, chewing on sweet-smelling mastic gum or sticks as they discuss legal affairs and societal needs of the community while scribes take note. Behind me, student priests clear away incense ashes and burn off the limestone altar to Yahu, the deity who freed our enslaved ancestors many suns ago. Male residents outnumber females here, so they do most of the chores—cleaning, farming, and even weaving and cooking.

A hot, dry, westerly breeze strokes my already warm

cheeks and sends scaly chaff of barley from the spring harvest floating into the morning's blue skies. Shadows of the thick, mudbrick walls, which rise some sixteen feet in the air and surround the village, cast cooling shade upon the corner of the inside gate where I wait, pulling down on the heavy iron rod of the open gatehouse wooden door to stretch out my back, still aching from yesterday's impromptu rescue.

I was in Geba, a town east of here—picking wild black mustard herbs that our chief cook, Tiye, wanted for Hag Hakhobez, a feast that starts in a few days—when a high-pitched moan took my attention. Caught in a grove of prickly shrubs was a little girl with blood-red welts over her skin, probably from mustard oil and branches, and dark purple bruises on her arms and legs, probably from the people who left her there. When I went into the thicket to liberate her, she thrust her hands at me, knocking me backward onto leaves and stems. I managed on the third try to pick her up and escape the pointy prison, then put her on my back, grabbed the bag of plants, and made the agonizing mile-long walk back to Ramah. The little one held tightly to my neck the entire way but never spoke a word. I named her Lo-Ruhamah, as she seemed unloved, like the two other children I had rescued over the last seven days.

My mother, our village healer, moved guardedly as she nursed Lo-Ruhamah's wounds with cardamon paste and bandages.

"It's not for us to interfere with another's family," she muttered again and again, as if she were in a daze. I decided to save my rebuttal for another day and simply promised not to bring another child to Ramah.

The rhythmic jingling of metal on metal brings me

back to the gatehouse. I hear what turns out to be gold rings before I can see them. The sound is liturgical, like the loud, hollow chirp of a chorus of giant shoebill storks from Misra'yim. Folks begin to gather near me—the elders, scribes, student priests, and my father.

"What's going on?" my father asks, his deep voice cutting through the commotion.

Most everyone honors my father as the high priest and last judge of the Ebre Y'israelites, people in twelve tribes now living across the central hill country of Kanaan, from the Y'hudah mounts in the south to the Shomron hills in the north. I call him Abbah, and his tall shadow adds extra shade to my head and back.

I continue my gaze at the gate as if I didn't hear his question, happy though that he's not wearing his formal high priest's tabernacle robe with its many small, gold bells and pomegranates along the hem that also clank and clack annoyingly. His everyday garb is much more subtle. A tan linen tunic reaches to his calves under a beige apron that hangs to his thighs. A broad leather belt sits at his waist. His signature mane of long, graying locs is untouched by a razor as it is the way of a Nazirite. At his chest hangs a thick gold chain that ends in an inch-tall gold cylinder amulet, containing a personal prayer written on a tiny sheepskin scroll given to him by his high priest predecessor, Eli.

A watcher at the gatehouse blows a tone on a ram's horn—one short, one long, two shorts. An approaching visitor.

The looming transport finally crests the hill, coming into view. It rolls through the front gate, barely missing people and animals, and makes a sharp circle so that it is heading back out.

Abbah steps closer to the young boy driver who straddles the two brown donkeys hitched to the long, narrow, wooden wagon mounted on four wooden-spoked wheels. Big brass bells adorn the animals' collars and saddles. Their cargo, I think, is a mule, though it's hard to tell. Its body is like a horse, but its longer head and ears are that of a donkey. It is larger than the donkeys that pulled it here, standing almost five feet tall at its shoulders, but it is slightly smaller than most mules I've seen. Its dull, off-white coat highlights dark, sunken eyes and a protruding rib cage. Twenty or more golden rings, strung together by indigo cords, swing all along the animal's scraggly head of hair and thin tail, putting more weight on its lanky legs.

A goat-skin holster, tied to the leather saddle on the equine, carries a silver sword that's about the length of my arm. A pocket on the other side of the saddle holds a gold goblet with elaborate etchings along its rim. The contradiction of pageantry and plain, plenty and poverty, clearly—and no doubt intentionally—expresses both the abundant wealth and boorishness of their sender.

Another boy—this one is skinnier with bold, brown eyes, full brown lips, and curly black hair—tenderly backs the horse-donkey down the wagon's ramps and, without saying a word, hands its reins to Abbah, along with a large sheepskin scroll tied with a long, purple ribbon. The second boy hops back on the wagon, the driver shouts to the donkeys, and they head back the way they came. Abbah watches them disappear before carefully unrolling the scroll and reading its message loud enough for the awaiting congregation to hear.

*To you, Adon Shmuel, high priest and oracle of
our people, the Eber Y'israelites,
I remain most delighted to take your daughter,
Abyga'el, as wife.
Let this rare breed stand as a sign of that bond,
Of obligatory gifts to you and the property to her
done.
In ten days, my ambassador will appear in Ramah
with glee.
To bring my bride to Ma'on, to me,
Where she will live and serve
Unnerved and with verve.
This I decree sincerely,
Adon Nabal
Of the house of Kaleb, tribe of Y'hudah.*

"Is this a joke?" Abbah asks slowly, still looking down at
the scroll.

Seeing after the spiritual and judicial affairs of our people
for more than seventy years, Abbah, son of Elqanah of the
tribe of Levi, has known all sorts of difficult situations—
enough, my mother mocks, to light a thousand bushes on fire
atop Mount Horeb at the same time without one of them
being consumed. But I have never seen such a bronze-hued
face turn so ashen as his is now.

"Tell me this is a joke," he commands, turning to me.

The yard is so quiet that you can hear the heat rising from
the pounded earth, even though a dozen or more people are
scattered around motionless, too shocked to move. The "rare
breed" horse-mule will likely be the symbol of my audacity
and imminent demise now that Abbah knows why it is here.

"It is as it says, Abbah," I manage to say while pains of
guilt ignite in my stomach in tiny yet intense convulsions,

like many needles. I regret letting him find out this way. "It is the final bride price from Nabal of Ma'on for . . . me."

"Come." Abbah barks, then hastens across the pebbled plaza, stepping over the ground drains and holes that collect sporadic rainwater. Given his long, strong legs even in his ninety years, Abbah strides strongly, easily, and swiftly past Yahu's altar, through the great and airy community meeting room at the village's center, to the narrow hallway behind the great room, and into his office secured by a thick, dark blue curtain. Hurrying to keep up with him, my breathing grows heavy and my legs tremble as he closes the drape behind me.

"Sit." He points to the cushion-topped bench opposite his desk as he clinches the back of his chair. "You are now the property of Nabal, and you don't even know him. Even worse, I don't know him. Explain."

"Well . . ." I take a deep breath, searching my mind for a suitable reason and a righteous response, but words are slow to emerge.

"Now, Aby," he orders. "How did this come to be?"

"Yes, well, it . . . it happened about two moons ago while you were on your national tour."

"Two moons ago?"

"Yessir. A messenger from the king delivered a marriage proposal." The many tribal and ritual objects around the room—both the elaborate and the primitive ones—seem to mock me with scorn and I feel a degree worse if that's possible.

"From Melek Shaul?"

"Yessir." The alarm on his face disturbs me. *Did I miss something?* "I, ah, received it on your behalf and put it there in the storage box with the others. I let Emah know that it had come."

"Your mother knew about this?"

"She only knew that another betrothal offer was made. I came back here the next day and read all the proposals. This one was the only one that promised land and it was already in contract form. I persuaded Noach to find out for me that the offeror owns hundreds of acres of land and thousands of cattle south of here. So, I made a few changes to the proposal, stamped it with your priestly seal, and sent it back."

Abbah presses his abdomen with his right hand and his usually plump lips purse together into a thin, tight line as if to keep the thoughts brewing in his mind from spewing out as wicked words. His eyes fix on the ceiling, avoiding me and mine. It is not his way. I don't get it. He should be thrilled, even proud of my becoming proactive to take decisive action and do what needs to be done.

"What are you trying to prove with these wild actions of yours? Without a thought beforehand. Without a care for the consequences. Without wise consideration of danger. You're smarter than this!"

"Abbah, I did not—"

"Trickery. Lies. Thievery. Such is not our way. Not Yahu's way. And it will not be tolerated, Aby, as it can only lead to chaos and death. You know this."

"Yessir."

"And understand that Noach is my deputy, my right hand," he says of the resident senior priest. "Noach serves me and the school. He is not subject to your impulses."

"Yessir," I acknowledge again.

"All this without my consent." He restarts his pacing, back and forth in front of the desk. "Unsanctioned by your parents."

Not my birth parents, but that is the starting point of

today's difficulty. "All due respect, Abbah, but I did not need your agreement."

"What did you say?"

"I am of adult age to take responsibility for my own actions."

"Have you lost your mind?" he screams and raises his hand toward me before slumping into his chair, near tears. "You may be of age, but I am your covering. I am the male to your female until there is a fitting male who replaces me. It is the divine order of things. You are barren of right sense to make this kind of vow, which is why you have a father."

"I thought—"

"No, you didn't think. That's the point. You didn't discuss this with me or Emah or anyone. You simply ignored my teaching to always get good counsel; to get a good understanding before making a decision. How I've told you repeatedly that we don't chase wealth; material value chases wisdom which you did not use in this case." He pauses to regather himself. "Aby, covenants are strategic moves for our people. We do not make them lightly. They must be done in truth and in the spirit of Yahu."

"But I went into the—"

"Did you once consider why this proposal came through the king's court? What does the offeror get besides you? Did his name not tell you anything about his nature? I have heard that he may have killed his own father to gain his abundance of land. Did Noach tell you that?"

The king's court? Nabal? A fool? Killed his father? Nothing like that occurred to me. The contract states his occupation as a sheepherder. Did it matter? Do I care? I might care.

"Well, I was foreto—"

"Did you consider that I might be in the process of

fulfilling my duty to negotiate a good future for you? A match much better than this? At what point did you ponder how your action would affect this house, *your* father, *your* mother, *our* family?" He slams his hand on the rugged wooden desk.

"I did get understanding and saw this as the best action." I lean in closer to him, knowing it best to stay seated. "You always told me that things don't just happen, they're made to happen, right? That's exactly what I did. I made a thing happen. I took the way revealed to me to do what I could do, just like you have always taught me. Just like you always do."

"You are not me, Aby, and there is much for you to learn. You have a father, so it is unnecessary for you to make such uncovered vows." He sits on the edge of his desk and his dark brown eyes soften a little. "The very thought of you being fixed to this fella is like sour grapes in my mouth. No amount of land is worth it, so it must be undone, and I will undo it."

"Undo it? Abbah, it cannot be undone." A deep knot clenches my throat as if I'd swallowed a raw fig whole.

"Cannot? Have you also forgotten who I am? There's nothing that Yahu and I cannot do. Leave me now so I may go within for relief and direction. I will deal with you and your actions later."

"Deal with me later? Abbah, I don't want this to be un—"

"Abyga'el." The chilly blast in Emah's voice is enough to halt my argument. "Leave us now." My mother's piercing eyes confirm her resolve and I trust that her speech will bear out the nature of her name. Zellah. My protection.

"And, Aby, tell no one about this," Abbah commands. "No one."

"How is that poss—"

"Now, Aby," Emah says with great strain.

Fine. Good. I'm happy to get out of here. The farther, the better. It makes no sense to try and reason with Abbah. What's done is done, and that's how I want it to stay. I trust that Emah will help him calm down and let it go.

"Wait!" Abbah calls out, putting my exit on pause. "You said that this was revealed to you?"

"Yessir?"

"How?"

"Precognition," Emah answers, directing Abbah's attention away from me. "Go, Aby."

I do as I'm told but stop on the right wall just outside the curtain to welcome the cool of smooth plaster on my back and to listen.

"Peace, Shmuel, peace." Emah is back to being the calm in a sudden storm. "Abyga'el has been having precognitive dreams for more than a year now."

"Zellah, why didn't you tell me?"

"Because the dreams she related to me were ordinary and vague. A sheep getting lost. A cloud over Ramah in summer. The scribe, Yetro, breaking his hand. For the most part, it was not much for the attention and only dim hints at second sight. But this one was different. Land below a healing sea. An uncommon gust from the south. Sunlight shimmering from the eyes of a little boy. Earth, water, wind, and fire. It got my attention. Some days later, Aby intercepted and read the offer of marriage from Nabal, then connected it to her vision before I knew about either one. I learned of the actual betrothal when you did. Just now. Am I furious? Yes. Am I disappointed? Of course. But this may very well be bigger than Aby and her high spirits."

"So, you think this one is a true dream? Foreknowledge?"

"It is becoming so every day."

They are quiet for a moment, and I have overheard enough. I leave to find the horse-mule in the animal stable. He looks the way I feel. Seems we both need to shake some anguish from the last few hours, so I make ready for a visit to Gan Aby, my self-proclaimed private garden of peace.

When I was seven, Emah and her two student servants from Abbah's priesthood school helped me flatten out a hilltop southeast of Ramah. I went back with others every day for a whole moon cycle. We built a small cistern to catch rainwater, planted greenery, made stone seating, and did other work to create my little piece of heaven. Being there under the pleasant veil of fig and terebinth trees will do me good. Me and the scrawny horse-mule.

We take our time walking the two miles in the open air and healing sunlight. Gan Aby is in full bloom, rich with fragrance from the terebinth's citrusy-scented yellowish flowers and its anise-odorous resin. Green and yellowing fruit of the sycamore-fig tree add hints of sweetness. Aromatically soothing, as always.

"Take in a big gulp of that," I instruct the animal as I do the same, releasing the breath slowly. He is drawn to the sycamore's bright-green, low-hanging, palm-shaped leaves and happily nibbles at them. I stroke his frail face and neck before wrapping his reins over a branch. I pick up my slingshot and stack my ammunition, then disguise and position my targets to start practice.

CHAPTER 2

BECKON

[beck-ōn]: to summon, signal, or appear inviting.

THERE IS A TIME TO KILL. That's what Abbah says when he's spouting off a list of times to do or not do things. Well, killing time is right here, right now, when I have that rat of an enemy to our people—a P'lishtim—dead center of my view. *Does he not know that I rule this area? Does he not fear the precision of my slingstones? It's time that I show him.*

The idiot intruder likely thinks that those dark, mossy feathers fanning out atop his brassy headgear camouflage him squatting among tamarisk bushes about a hundred yards away from where I stand. They don't. They only serve as a trail to the wrinkly tension in his forehead, the tight squint of his sneaky eyes, and the lone crease in his broad nose. It is a mess of a burnt orange face, still roasting in the desert heat.

Keeping an eye on him from my own hiding place, I reach slowly into my side holster and pull my sling, which is already damp from my sweat after hours of practice. I pause a second to thank the sycamore-fig tree for the pleasantry of its hefty crown of teeming branches. For about the hundredth time this morning, I slide a smooth claystone—about two inches in diameter—into the leather cradle of my sling. I take in my left hand the two long cords of braided wool connected to each end of the cradle, causing the stone to sway back and forth in its cot like a gold hoop dangling from the dainty ear of a young dancer. With my right hand, I pull the cradle with its precious cargo straight out and level to the ground to ready it for takeoff. Left elbow bent. One underhanded rotation. Once more for greater speed. A flick of the wrist, a whistle, and a quick release of the cord. The stone shoots out of the cradle in a spin, barely making a sound as it slices the air. *Swoosh! Smack! Whack!* Flawless. The enemy's head splits open, gushing out moist golden meat, stringy pulp, and seeds. That pumpkin of a giant, pork-eating P'lishtim is dead. A virtuous kill. Even for a girl.

I load up the sling again. My next target is a beady-eyed Ammonite gourd, another one of our enemies, that is crouching to my right. A smooth stone. A loop of the straps. A start of the windup. A whistle. Just as the second rotation enters its downswing, the sound of crunching dry earth seizes my attention. I turn around quickly toward the interruption and see the silhouette of a person strapped with at least one weapon. A man. I can't be sure, but with rumblings of discord coming from the Eber capital of Gibeah not that far from here, I can't take the chance. On sheer instinct, I wind up and quickly release my missile. *Swoosh!* The intruder falls flat to the ground a second before the stone zooms over him. *Thwack! Crack!* The stone smashes into a tree. I start to wind up again.

"Whoa, girl. Watch where you send that thing." The stranger yells in a muddled voice. Being face down in the dirt makes clear speech difficult. He raises his chest and yells again, "Stand down and fix that sorry aim. You could kill Eber royalty. Look first. Spot your target. Then, shoot. Surely, I taught you to sling better than that!"

Dawit? I step backward in both hesitancy and hope. *Could it be?* The near victim stands up slowly. Tall. Dark. Muscular. High knotted, turban headwrap on his head. "Dawit?"

"Hush, girl. Only Yahu knows what enemy could be near."

"DAHHHWWHHEATTTTTTT." I run to him and jump onto his warm chest. My arms clasp around his neck, dragging down his colorful headwrap and freeing his locs to massage my face. I cling to him tightly. Not even a gentle breeze could pass between us. *He is here. He. Is. Here.*

His frame is bigger than I remember. His scent, though—frankincense, calamus, and cinnamon with a bit of sweaty musk—is unforgettable. So is the incitement swelling up from my femininity, even more than it did two years ago.

I was thirteen. Emah and I had arrived in Gibeah, the capital city of our people and home to our king, Shaul. We were there for the wedding of Michal, the king's youngest daughter, who was given to Dawit in marriage to satisfy the king's publicly announced bride price: the foreskins of one hundred P'lishtim. Dawit, being a self-sacrificing and dutiful warrior, brought two hundred. Such feats earned him the people's hearts and praise, and the king's jealousy.

Abbah delayed joining us. He was on his "re" trip, as Emah called it in her lament about its *re*-volving nature. Twice a year, Abbah toured key Eber Y'israel cities, visiting tribal chiefs and local leaders, settling disputes, and delivering justice. It was how Yahu's order and decency stayed somewhat top of mind among us. If needed, he would *re*-forecast the future of Y'israel—her rise, if she obeys and honors Yahu, or her ruin if she doesn't. Her return to slavery by ship. Disease of every kind. Blown to every corner of the earth. A part of every culture in the world yet without her own, and other horrid conditions. Listeners *re*-vowed to walk the path of light, *re*-joicing in song and dance. As soon as Abbah left their presence, many would *re*-turn to whatever evils they enjoyed before his arrival and wander along the path of curses which meant he had to *re*-visit them and do it all over again. Emah *re*-solved that she and I would no longer go with Abbah on the "re" trips.

Emah and I had settled our belongings in what the king's domestics called "the prophet's room." A smaller and humbler version of the king's palace, it is a three-level house within the royal fortress, hidden behind a fence of oak trees that stand like soldiers, some thirty feet high. It is where Abbah always stayed during his advisements to Shaul. Young servants scurried around us like desert ants, hastily turning here and there to fan burning incense, fill bathing jugs, light oil lamps, and attend to any other little thing just to keep busy. The scampering made my body itch all over, so I decided to go to the rooftop for relief.

At the edge of the walled mudbrick roof, I inhaled a cool desert breeze and gazed at the twilight's full moon. Underneath the looming moonlight, I saw what looked like a man with his feet tied together at the trunk of one of the trees. His arms were outstretched and tied to nearby branches. Several round stones, about the size of a large melon, were littered about the bottom of the tree. Head down, the prisoner seemed too wounded to make a sound, which is probably why I had not noticed him.

Another man stood about six feet in front of the hanging

man, his back to me, holding a stone at the center of his chest. The standing man pumped his legs twice in a rocking-like motion, then suddenly projected the stone to the dead center of the weak man's stomach, causing his body to shake.

I jetted forward, palms sweaty and heart pounding, nearly falling off the roof. I balanced myself onto the ledge, leaped onto a fat tree limb nearby, crawled down its rough bark to the ground, and crept among the trees until I got close to the strong man. When he squatted down to pick up a stone, I rushed in and knocked him down. My chest landed on his back. And there it was. Frankincense, calamus, and cinnamon, with a bit of sweaty musk. Dawit, practicing his stone-throwing skills on a dummy figure made to look like a man. I rolled onto the ground, wanting to bury myself in it. He lifted me up with deep groans and gritted teeth.

"Abyga'el?" Dawit's voice snaps me back to now. "Is it really you?"

"Yes." I exhale into the back of his neck on my tiptoes, still clinging to him. What feels like an hour has only been a few moments. "It is me."

"I can hardly believe it. Let me see." He unshackles my grasp and I fall away. His eyes examine me from head to toe. Mine does likewise to him.

His sleeveless, at-the-knee linen tunic leaves his arms and legs free for flight or fight and highlights his unique array of blue tassels: two of typical length at the side seams, four shorter ones in the front, and four shorter ones in the back. I have never seen a tunic with tassels all along the hem like that. A rod of oak tied to his battle belt hangs past his calf and his goat-hair sling rests on his hip. No doubt, the slingstones are at hand. Thick leather footboards are strapped to his feet with thin leather thongs.

"My, oh my. Look at you. You were just a youngling climbing trees when I last saw you in Gibeah and taught you the sling and other war skills in between my betrothal duties." He does remember that awkward encounter and even another one years earlier when I was about six and on a tour with Abbah.

"Now, you're . . . you're . . . you're different." He blushes boldly. "Taller and slimmer and, dare I say, shapelier. How it is that you turned into such a glorious beauty in only a few cycles of the moon?"

"A few cycles of the moon? What moon cycles have you been counting? It's been almost two earth revolutions around the sun since we were in the capital for your wedding."

"Really? You're probably right. Well, they surely have been good to you, girl. I have never seen such loveliness among Eber Y'israelites." Now I'm blushing. No doubt, he sees it but keeps talking anyway. "I'm sure the old man is burdened down with betrothal requests for you, but oh, maybe you're already married? I wouldn't at all be surprised."

"No and no." I assert quickly, not wanting to go near that topic. "What are you doing here?" As soon as the words leave my mouth, I hear the same crackling of dry earth behind Dawit. Three other men about two hundred yards away are walking toward us. "Get down," I whisper and quickly reach for my sling. He bends down while turning around to spy the danger.

"No, Aby!" Dawit yells, while grabbing my wrist. "Stop!"

"What?" I hiss in confusion, crouching down beside him. "It could be trouble. Someone followed you here."

"Hang up your weapon, Abyga'el. They are with me." Dawit stands and faces the men who are close enough to hear him.

"No need to fear," Dawit calls to them.

"Are you sure, Dah?" one of the men counters, cautiously examining me. "It would be a damn shame for us to escape Gibeah just to die a half day's walk away in Ramah."

"Yeah, Dah . . ." another says. "We could end up like those sad gourds over there." They look in the direction of my disfigured foes and burst into laughter. "Rad, didn't we kill that guy three moons ago?" They roar even louder.

"Yeah, bruhs, I'm sure," Dawit reassures, emptying his last chuckle. "We're fine and in good hands. This beautiful maiden is Abyga'el, daughter of Shmuel, the high priest, and one of Eber Y'israelites' sweetest lambs. Don't let your guard down too low, though. She is fierce on the sling."

"What you say is surely true, Dah," the tallest one says and stares at me. "We can clearly see it."

"Aby . . ." Dawit continues, "This is Raddai and Ozem, older seeds of Yishai, our father. Lesser seeds, I might add."

"Lesser in your mind, bruh; only in your mind," Raddai says with a handsome smile that accentuates his square jaw. He stands over six feet and has a Dawit-like face atop a muscular build that's covered in skin the color of golden-brown dates. Ozem is slightly shorter, browner, and heavier, with deep, friendly eyes that sparkle like polished black onyx.

"Peace be upon you, my sister," they say almost in unison, nodding to me.

"And unto you, my brothers," I reply, still blushing unwillingly for no reason that pleases me. *Get it together, girl. Get it together.*

"And this young one here"—Dawit grabs the neck of the slender man, about my age, who is lanky with high cheekbones and little facial hair—"is my scout. He is Kurib, seed of Labayu. May Yahu be pleased with him." Dawit grins and slaps the man on his back. Kurib looks more like a schoolteacher or a priest in training rather than the warrior ensemble around him.

"Peace," he says with a flash of a smile that quickly disappears.

"Peace." I smile back then turn to Dawit. "You need a spy these days?"

"Unfortunately, but let's not talk about me. Let's talk about you. What of you since Gibeah?"

"As you can see, I perfected the sling . . ."

"Oh, maybe gotten more aggressive, but perfect?" He examines my hands for marks. "I'd say not. There are still a few tricks I can teach you."

"I'm sure." I nod in humble agreement. "Before your grand entrance, I was just about to have a meal. Care to join me?"

"Absolutely." Ozem does not hesitate to answer. "But first, allow me to take out that last dog."

"As you wish, my lord," I permit, bouncing out of his way. "As you wish."

He unhinges his bow from his shoulder holster and pulls an arrow from the quiver on his back. With his left side aligned with the foe, he slides the arrow's notch into the bowstring and raises the weapon to his chest. His sleeve droops, revealing his bulging muscles. He pulls back the bow, aims at the target, and releases the arrow. *Twang! Swoosh! Craaack!* The squash head splits open, spilling seeds and goo on the ground.

"And that's how you win a battle," he says with finality.

"Who—or should I say what—is that?" Dawit points to the hungry horse-mule, still chomping on leaves.

"Oh, that's . . . that's my new horse-mule," I blurt out.

"Your what?"

"My part horse, part mule transport."

"Is he breaking a forty-day fast?" Raddai hoots and they all begin chuckling again.

"No, no. I, uh, just rescued him from his owner who treated him cruelly," I voice my reasonable explanation. "Laugh now, but just wait until I bring him back to his glory. You'll all want him for your own, but I will never allow it." The horse-mule whinnies squeakily and nods his head as if he understands our banter.

"I have no doubt," Dawit says. "Hold on." He trots to his donkey and comes back with a kidskin bag full of bread, olives, dried fruits, and a gourd for keeping water. A much longer rod, also of oak, hangs on his animal. "Let us dine."

They rest their gear, and we sit on stone seats under the shady trees in my heaven. I have more than enough roasted barley, raw figs, flatbread, vinegar dip, hyssop water, and raisin cake to silence hungriness.

"You're not at the king's palace," I slur, wiping sweet fig pulp from my mouth. "He kicked you out?"

"More like I ran out, but again, that's a topic for another time."

"Okay, then, next topic: Why do you have a metal clip on your ear?"

"Oh, this," he grins and slides off the gold tubular cuff from the upper part of his left ear and hands it to me. "See the head of rams all along the curve?"

"Yeah. Nice," I say. "Why?"

"We all have the ram in some form or another," Ozem chimes in and shows me his ring. Raddai and Kurib flaunt their pendants.

"It is a quick and easy way for us to identify those in our rare little band of refugees." Dah resets his ear clip.

"A band of . . . rams," I whisper, remembering the story of our ancestral fathers Ab-Raham and Yitshak, and the ram representing sacrifice, protection, and guidance. "Couldn't a foe simply make his own to deceive you?"

"Not like this," Raddai adds. "We placed a special mark on our metal stamp that only we know and can identify."

"The ram band," I proclaim.

"Clever," Kurib, the quiet guy, says. "With that sling strength of yours, one day you might be one of us."

"Twilight is 'bout gone . . ." Dah says as he looks to the sky, "making way for a new day. And without the benefit of moonlight, I think it's time for us roving rams to go into the fold and feed on the good pasture of the old man. Agreed?"

"Yes," I agree. "No doubt, Emah already has her favorite platter prepared for my head for missing my curfew."

CHAPTER 3

BELONG

*[be-lōng]: to be attached or bound
by birth, allegiance, or dependency.*

OIL LAMPS BURN ALONG THE RIM of Ramah's guarded walls and gatekeepers watch folks' coming and going. Priests-in-training play a board game just inside the gate under the light of lamps. They are two of about a hundred males, aged twelve to eighteen, who help meet the needs of the village as part of their six-moons probation before attending the school for priests in Naoith, a hamlet about three miles north of here. There, they train in what Abbah calls "spiritual things" that prepare them to serve as seers, priests, and prophets for the Ebre Y'israelite nation. A senior principal of the school strolls the yard. He recognizes Dawit and falls to his knees before him.

"No, brother." Dawit interlocks his right arm with the man's right arm, helping him up. "No call for that, please. We are one and I am your ready servant." The provost seems pleased, gleaming with delight.

"Hey, gorgeous old woman!" Dawit spots Emah and hurries to her.

"If you see an old woman, give her a long-overdue hug," she jokes. He picks her up and spins her around and around. She squeaks and squeals and giggles. More people come out to investigate the ruckus. Dawit and my youngest brother, Abiyah, embrace one another with kisses on their cheeks. Others pat Dawit on the back and ask about his recent battles and victories, being already intrigued by the infamous slayer of the giant and the so-called lion of the Eber tribe, Y'hudah. Dah manages to introduce his entourage in between inquiries.

"Where is the old man?" Dawit looks around at the faces in the crowd.

"He is in isolation right now, fasting and praying," Emah answers. "He may be done by morning, and I know he'll be thrilled to see you."

"As I will him."

"Our brother has finally returned to Ramah after a very long absence and with exhaustion on his face," Abiyah says as Emah clutches Dawit's arm. "Go and prepare water for washing, food for nourishment, and resting places for good sleep for our visitors." The student servants scamper off.

"At tomorrow's twilight," Emah announces for all to hear, "we will make ready to celebrate your homecoming in true Eber style as we also observe new moon, yes?"

"Yes," Dawit answers. "May it be as you have said, Emah Zellah and Akhi Abiyah."

Servants escort Dawit and his crew to their sleeping rooms and I scurry to my room to freshen up, intending to help serve food to our special visitors.

With Dawit being here, the girl in the bronze-shone mirror looking back at me seems inadequate. Her long, black, coiling hair is thick and wild. Her full lips are dull and crackly. Her chestnut skin is dry and dusty. Her brown eyes appear gray. *How is it that he called her "beautiful"?* Had I better heeded Emah's instruction to use balsam oil on my hair and cleanse my face with honey and lemon, then maybe I'd look more like the daughter of a king rather than the son of a pauper. It's too late to make a big difference now. I wash my face, tie a scarf around my hair, and wet my lips before walking back toward the community house.

"A daughter of this house knows to be in by sundown," Emah intercepts my trek. "Yes?"

"Yes, Emah, I know. It's just that when Da—"

She holds up her right hand, signaling me to stop talking. I do so, immediately.

"Just because an unexpected event interrupts your plan doesn't mean you abandon it or break home protocols. What if it wasn't Dawit walking up on you, but some Y'israelite enemy?"

"I had my sling and even used it on Dawit. Ask him."

"Maybe. But next time, find a way to adapt and maintain house rules. Otherwise, you'll have an escort going forward. Understand?"

"Yes, ma'am," I accept, attempting to satisfy her motherly duty so we can move on. "So why do you call him son and say that he's home?"

"Dawit?"

"Yes."

"Home is in the heart, not in a place. Over the past eight years or so, Dawit has become a kindred spirit with your father and me. He and Abbah are a lot alike. Bold and brave. Forward thinking. Caring. Intuitive, impatient, and impulsive, like you." A warm smile flavors her face. "Even though we don't see him much anymore, he is like a son to us and belongs here too. Wherever we are is home to him—no different than Yo'el, Abiyah, or you."

"Does that mean that he and I are siblings too?"

"Could be. It's just that he's a son to us, not necessarily a brother to you. Why?"

"Ah, no reason. Just asking."

"Oh, no."

"What?"

"I know this look and you dare not have it," she surveys my face. "You dare not have it, girl. The vow that you already made puts you way past it, so don't have it, don't see it, don't feel it."

"I don't know what you mean."

"You know exactly what I mean, and you are unavailable for it. You may as well do as you said earlier and consider Dawit your brother. Understand me?"

"Yes, ma'am." I do understand, but do not agree. A feeling of shame or regret or some other uncomfortable sentiment rises from my throat. "Still, can we not tell him about my, ah, situation? I don't want him to know about the betrothal."

Her reply is lagging. "Tell no one. That is the order we both received from Abbah. I'm sure he instructed the same throughout Ramah because he is determined to undo it. So, there may be nothing to tell. For now, go back to your room and go to sleep. We have much to do tomorrow."

"But it's still early and I was on my way to help with the service for our visitors."

"No. Not tonight. Go back to your room, do something with that woolly bush on your head, and forget what you are thinking about Dawit."

I wake the next morning well before dawn, roll up my bed, and sit still, greeting Yahu and imagining the day I want. As I step out into the dim morning, lamppost lights cast long shadows on my side of the inner village wall. Five men ride through the back gate. *Abbah, Dawit, and Dah's crew. Oh well.*

I commence doing the few chores that I have, starting with making the fire in the clay oven for baking bread. I restock firewood, then help grind daily grain, legumes, and lentils, and store them in shelf jars and ground pits for the cooks' use. Lastly, I tend to the animals.

Our flock of fifty or so sheep and goats roam the south side of the village on the thirty-foot-wide trench in between the double guard walls. This part of the mostly dry channel is an enclosed grassy terrace with a small, man-made stream trickling through it that provides water and safe grazing space when student priests don't take the herd out to roam larger fields. Stalls within a stone shelter in the courtyard, also on the south side, house asses and a camel. Mangers in each stall hold water and food. I help keep the stalls clean, the mangers full, and the animals healthy.

The horse-mule is my last patient. I brush his patchy coat, being careful around his bruises, burns, and wounds, and causing hair to fly all around me. He seems to like it and grazes my shoulder with his nose.

"Curse your tormentors. They were most unkind to you, weren't they? Was it that fool, Nabal?"

He lets out a loud whinny that makes me jump back.

"So, you do speak," I smile. "No need to fear the fool anymore. You are where you belong. With me." I wipe him with cedarwood and myrrh oils to cleanse, heal, and brighten his coat. I add flax seeds, coriander seeds, and sprouted wheat to his hay to balance his gut and ease his mouth and body odor.

"No one told me your name, though I'm sure you have one. But since I do not know it, I will give you a new name. You will be known as Uziyah because no matter how you may feel in this moment, Yahu is always your power and strength." *Yes, that feels right.* He nods his head, seeming to agree. "Uziyah. Yes. Uzi for short. Yahu made you beautifully sturdy. You are amazingly tough with unmatched wit and intelligence. You are the envy of all other animals." I rub his back. He nods and bumps me with his nose. *Strange.* Strange enough to be my cue to finish up and go over to the food house for first meal.

As usual, flatbread is baking in outdoor ovens lit by my fire, beckoning those working on the estate to come and eat. I wash my hands and face, then go in. Priests, students, and other residents are scattered about, but no Abbah. No Dawit. No ram band. I gobble up warm bread with pulpy apricot honey on top without really tasting it, then head back out.

"Gebirah Abyga'el?" Tiye, our chief cook, calls after me. The only thing dwarfing her small frame is her bold, sassy, take-charge attitude. She beckons me back with her left hand. Her resolute I-ain't-playing hand wields a tattoo of eight black dots with dashes in between running from her wrist to her middle finger. Her father made it with charcoal ink, Tiye once told me, when she was eight years old for her to remember the slavery of her people in Misra'yim and for her to be servant to Yahu only, rather than her flesh. She says it keeps her humble with a side of fierceness. It stands out brilliantly against her rich golden hue, the color of wheat just before harvest. "Where do you think you're going in such a hurry with all the fixings to be done 'round here?"

"Ma'am?"

"The firewood? The mill? The flock?"

"All done."

"All done? Hard to believe. When?"

"Early. Very early, after a good night's sleep."

"Un-huh," she gripes and dashes away to check the food storage containers. "Well, well, well. You did do it. Chile, you not dying or moving away or nothing, are you?" She watches me, her hands on her hips.

"Uhhh, no, ma'am." *Does she mean the betrothal?*

"Un-huh. I know why you cleared your day. Un-huh, it's him, ain't it? He ain't here. Un-huh. He left with the high priest a long time ago and ain't no telling when they'll be back. Ain't no telling, so you just go on 'bout your day and do something else."

"What? Oh, ah, no. I . . . I . . . I just want to practice the sling so, you know, I can get better at it."

"Un-huh. We'll see how long that lasts," she says with mockery in her voice. "Go on, girl."

I wrap up some raisin cakes and melons, pack Uzi for riding, and then head out.

"Let's try out these legs again," I say to him. He's a tad wobbly when I climb on but he pins his ears in determination and quickly sturdies up. "Good boy."

"*Tweeeeet-tweeeeet-kola-kola-tweet-tweet-kola-tweeeeet,*" Uzi makes a high-pitched whistle noise as he nods and kicks up his right foot. Startled, I slip right off his back and my butt hits the ground. *What just happened?*

"What?" I get up and walk around to look into his eyes. "You understand me, don't you?"

"*Tweeeeet-tweeeeet-kola-kola-tweet-tweet-kola-tweeeeet.*" He kicks again.

"Oh my," I whisper to him. "Yahu indeed can bear

miracles out of misery. Though we both are scarred by those who should have loved us, we are fierce and can overcome what others throw at us. There is much for us to devise and do." We must look ridiculous or suspicious; me, talking to his face and him, just standing there in the middle of the courtyard. "Let's do so in private in Gan Aby, huh?"

CHAPTER 4

BELOVE

*[be-luv]: an intense emotion of affection,
warmth, fondness, and regard toward a person or thing.*

WHEN WE GET TO THE GATEHOUSE, Abbah and the others are returning.

"Peace, Abbah and all," I say.

"Aby." Abbah is still cold with me. Hopefully, the benefit of his isolation and meditation will kick in soon. The others greet me with enthusiasm.

"Where are you going?" Dawit asks.

"Back to Gan Aby, the garden where we were yesterday."

"Gan Aby?"

"My own little piece of heaven on earth. Perhaps, I can sway you to come with me and teach me more about the sling? I mean, only if you feel up to it, of course."

"I'm always up to helping a beautiful girl in need, and if I tell the truth—and I always do—you need to improve your precision. A lot." He smiles and taps me on my shoulder. "Let's go and shoot some more enemy gourds."

"Be back before sundown," Abbah instructs. "We have much to celebrate tonight."

The ride to Gan Aby becomes a playful test of will. I dare to pit the pace of my fragile Uzi against Dah's donkey in a sprint. Uzi wins, though I don't know how. I give him extra melon for his gallant effort despite his weak condition. Maybe Dah let us win, but I will never concede that.

The rest of our afternoon is spent on the sling and the various whirling techniques and ammunition types to extend my range and sharpen my accuracy.

Dah stands in front of me with his head to the side and one eyebrow raised higher than the other before he speaks, "Why do you whistle before your release?"

"Whistle?"

"Yes. Right before you release the stone, you pucker your mouth and whistle."

"Really? I didn't know that."

"Well, now you do."

"Is it a problem?"

"I doubt that it hinders your skill, but it will alert your target so consider if you want to be that nice. If not, then work on it."

Perfectionist.

We continue to practice for a bit longer and then rest, finding relief in the shade of trees and some lemon water.

"Have you come across any abandoned children or runaways during your travels around Kanaan?" I wonder if he has heard of the rescues.

"Once, when I was keeping my father's sheep in outer Bet Lekhem, I came across a little boy near death," Dah pauses, his eyes tearing. "He did end up dying, I'm saddened to say. After that period, I spent most of my time serving Shaul near the palace or warring in the woods or city edges where children are not found. Why do you ask?"

"I hear that children are surely being found in the woods, at city edges, and many places in between. They are severely lashed or maimed or left on the street or worse as chastisement, all in accordance with Moshe's law."

"No, that's horrible and not in accordance with Moshe's law. I'd say it's the abusers' interpretation of the law." Dah seems to be as troubled about this news as I am.

"Abusers and judges, apparently."

"I haven't seen where the law gives its authority to such cruelty."

"It's a problem that's akin to burning our children in fire to our god, like our neighbors do."

"Might that have something to do with rumors about people putting yellow thread on their windows or trees to protect children? Have you heard about that?"

"Mmm . . . maybe." I would rather avoid that topic.

"I know nothing of it myself and doubt that it's true. Speaking of children in distress, did you get in trouble with Emah Zellah yesterday?"

"First, I'm not a child." I would rather hope he had noticed that much.

"Clearly."

"And second, not too much. She gave me a talking to and warned me about the consequences if I am ever that late again."

"It won't happen again, not on my watch."

"Your watch? Funny."

"Yeah, girl. As long as I'm here, I'm holding your butt accountable. You best know it." He chuckles and leans against a tree. "You know, I could get used to this."

"Being all sweaty, practicing the sling most of the day?" I slide down next to him.

"Nah. Lounging in Gan Aby with you. What will really sweeten it up, though, is a butterfly oasis. That's what we should build here next."

"We? What's this 'we'?"

"Yes, we. You and me. We can put some flowering black-bindweed, hyssop, and milkweed plants there, near the date palm trees. Add a big pot with sand and water in it and sprinkle more of that gravel around it. And that's it. Then, butterflies will come and relax here too."

"Just how do you know all this?"

"I know more than war and looking good, girl. Trust me." He grins. "I learned a lot about creation and some of the smallest creatures during the many days and nights I spent watching over my father's flock. Did you know that harvester ants collect grains and grind the seeds into a kind of bread, like ours, that they store in their nests?"

I shake my head as he turns to face me. "Or did you know that your big, golden-brown eyes—the prettiest among women—mimic what happens when a bright star blasts out of its glowing outer layers into cool air, creating a round, elaborate, fan-like design around the star?"

"So, you're a warrior and a weed?" I shake my head again before he reaches out for my hand, and I extend it. He turns up my palm.

"Did you know that the palm of this beautiful hand doesn't darken, even in the Kanaan sun? And these fingers . . ."—he strokes each one—"do not have muscles. They are controlled by muscles here," he touches my palm again, "and here." He moves his fingers along my forearm. My breathing speeds up. "And those plump, tawny, deeply defined lips of yours never perspire because they do not have sweat or oil glands." His mouth is so close to mine that its sweetness tickles my nose. I want to raise up so that mine meets his, but instead, I roll to my left and tumble to the ground.

"I, ah, well . . ."

"Oh, oh." He helps me up. "My apologies, Aby, if my truth or my attraction offends you."

"Oh, ah, no. Not . . . at . . . all. It's just that the, ah, sun is—"

"Yes, of course."

We agree that the sun is telling us to leave Gan Aby now to arrive at Ramah before the wall lamps glow.

I go straight to my room, longing for that missed kiss. Heat still pulsates from my womanhood at the idea of knowing Dah as my beloved, a mental and physical place that's new to me. The curious girl in the mirror desires it, but with more shimmery skin, pleasing lips, magnetic eyes, and well-arranged hair. I do what I can with what I have. Massage two drops of olive oil into my face. Pomegranate seed oil on my lips. Coils dressed in rosemary and grapeseed oils then collected high up into a bun, held together by a scarf of many bright colors.

Shortly after twilight, I join all the other Ramahans in the inner courtyard. Several water basins offer facilities for ritual face, hand, and foot washing. Fire flames crackle and pop from the many wall torches and tree lamps scattered about to illuminate our gathering. Senior priests wait in the gatehouse towers. As soon as they hear a long, faint horn blast from Gibeah announcing the dark of the rising moon, they echo it by sounding the ram's horn in Ramah. Student priests on the ground then light fires on the hillsides behind Ramah and burn dried flowers of the blue lotus plant to calm minds, beckon euphoria, cast floral scents into the air, and encourage high spiritual encounters.

"Hear, Eber Y'israelites," Abbah hushes the people and starts the festivities with his oration. Shouts of praise ripple through the congregation. "Yahu is our God. Yahu, the one God, alone. Tonight, the light of a new moon soon returns. It is the second great and faithful witness in the heavens to the enormity of Yahu, our great creator and sustainer. Thank you, Yahu, for moons past and gone. Thank you for this new time, further awareness, and steady order through this new moon. We lay old hearts and minds on your altar and reckon clean hearts, renewed minds, vigorous strength, bright opportunities, and new mercies so that we may do what is right and good in your sight and enjoy a long and abundant life. Now, everyone, raise your cup and drink anew as we enter this new moon feast together."

We drink the wine in our cups and take seats on color-ful mats and cushions that surround low, cloth-covered tables and crates. Tiye's kitchen attendants place upon them huge platters of spongy flatbread topped with yellow and red lentil stews, spiced chickpea chowder, roasted onions, leeks, dandelion greens, and pitted pick-led olives. We scoop the vegetables with the spongy bread and eat it by hand, often feeding one another as expressions of family intimacy while discussing our vari-ous hopes, dreams, and gratitude, which brings Uzi to my mind. I sneak away to surprise him with a bowlful of ol-ives, which he likes.

"*Tweet, kola, kola.*" I've already forgotten the special signal we've been working on. He ignores it, putting his attention on the olives.

"I'll keep working on it, okay?"

He stares at me as he chews.

"I know. It's a little different." I touch my face and hair

scarf. "Just sprucing up a little bit more, you know, for our special guests. Don't worry, though. I am aware that I am under contract, but I have everything under control. Just know that it is my heart that matters most to me, and it is still free to choose, thank you very much." He continues to stare. *Am I trying to convince him or me? I must be delusional, talking to the horse-mule as if he has an opinion one way or the other. Help me, Yahu. Help me.*

When I return to the feast, the many chatters have died down to the one talk taking place at the table where Abbah, Noach, Dawit, and a few others are seated. Most everyone else shifts our seating around them.

"And now we have Shaul's kingship," Abbah says. "And as Yahu predicted when the people first asked for a king, it is increasingly focused on a corrupt and dictatorship agenda rather than obedience to Yahu's order and service to the people. It's a reflection of a polluted mind."

"Right, and a mind being driven by fear," Rad adds. "And the people who support him do so because of fear."

"Fear of what?" Noach asks.

"Fear of failure, of losing fame, of losing significance," Rad answers. "All of which is happening because of his own behavior. Telling lies. Breaking laws, like taking holy artifacts from the temple and storing them in the palace. And doing all manners of self-centered evil that strikes at the life and freedoms of his own people. And blaming everyone except himself."

"That's the only one he's faithful to, himself," Kurib adds. "He shuts down and denigrates any opposers, even his own proven loyalists."

"That's certainly what he's trying to do to me," Dah agrees. "I figured out that the bride-price to marry his daughter—the foreskins of one hundred P'lishtim—was simply a ruse for me to be killed. When it didn't happen by the hand of the P'lishtim, Shaul moved to do it himself. Even as I was soothing his vile spirit with music like he asked, he threw a spear at me. Twice, I had to dodge his attempts. He then ordered his son, Yonathan, and his servants to kill me, but Yonathan warned me and found a way to change his father's mind. Even still, Shaul sent men to my house to kill me, but I escaped through a window and came here. All this, without cause as I remain faithful to Yahu, if not Shaul himself."

"Disappointing," Abbah says, looking down. "Extremely disappointing. The last time I was with Shaul, I was chastising him for disobeying Yahu's instructions to kill all the Amalekites during war. That was ten earth revolutions ago. The more I tried to show him his slide away from Yahu, the less he could see it. His excuse was the people or other nations, seeing the cause of his troubles coming from outside of him rather than from within his own heart. What I'm hearing from you is that he refuses to repent and is becoming as a mad wolf, inciting the uprisings of fools."

"Not as a mad wolf, is a mad wolf," Dah says. "I've seen that madness up close."

"It is that kind of misguided vanity that, if not rooted out, will draw upon us curses rather than blessings. We will end up scattered around the world far away from Kanaan, back into slavery but by ships, worshipping the god of our captors, and hanging as strange fruit on peculiar trees in foreign lands while children of a false Ab-Raham occupy our father's tent." The corners of Abbah's mouth drop and his eyes begin to water as if he is funeralizing his best friend.

"Yahu forbids," Abiyah exclaims. "Why would you say that, Abbah?"

"I'm not saying it. Yahu said it and it is already written and it is of our own choosing whether we realize it or not."

"Could one man's vainglorious behavior actually cause those things to happen to Yahu's Y'israel?"

"Indeed, it can, and it will if it is not stopped and if enough of Eber Y'israel follow suit." Quiet seeps over the setting for a moment, leaving only the sad, haunting hoot of an owl, like a moan.

"Dah, what did your wife think about what was happening to you at the palace?" I gasp as the question jumps out of my mouth before I can stop it. I feel the stares of many judging eyes at my inappropriately familiar and delicate ask. "Oh, forg—"

"Nothing to forgive. We are family. I suspect that my wife is no longer my wife, considering her father's perception of me." Dah looks off in a strained wonder, possibly mulling over what may be happening with the king's daughter. "There wasn't really anything Michal could think or do. Like the rest of us in Shaul's court, she saw the folly in her father and when I needed to run for my life, she risked her own to help me escape. Basically, I left her and pray daily that she is kept safe and sane."

"Well, we are thankful for her and that you are here where you belong," Abbah says, his spirit seeming loftier, lighter.

"Yes, Abbah, and I am happy to be here, celebrating with all of you underneath a newly created moon that is bringing to us, if only for this night, new hope for peaceful days ahead." Dawit picks up his lyre and begins to play.

CHAPTER 5

BEHOLD

[be-hōld]: to gaze upon.

THE FINGERS OF DAWIT'S RIGHT HAND strum the lower half of the instrument's ten strings that hover over the hollow wood sound box while those of his left hand, seemingly suspended in the air, work behind the lyre to orchestrate the top half of the strings. All ten flutter in a swift, intoxicating dance that compels me to jiggle. Ozem steadies a drum between his knees and starts up an accompanying beat. I grab my timbrel just as Abbah calls up a spiritual chant, to which we all respond festively.

Ohhhhh, oh, oh, oh! Ohhhhh, oh, oh, oh!
Ahhhhh, ah, ah, ah! Ahhhhh, ah, ah, ah!

Your lunar sign gives us your time.
To reawake with new minds, that in oneness we shine.
With the colored new moon sky, renew our unseen eye.
So, we lift our voices and cry,

Ohhhhh, oh, oh, oh! Ohhhhh, oh, oh, oh!
Ahhhhh, ah, ah, ah! Ahhhhh, ah, ah, ah!

As dark night flees the coming light,
Let fresh beginnings stir yonder heights.
With the colored new moon sky, renew our unseen
eye.
So, we lift our voices and cry,

Ohhhhh, oh, oh, oh! Ohhhhh, oh, oh, oh!
Ahhhhh, ah, ah, ah! Ahhhhh, ah, ah, ah!

With the colored new moon sky, renew our unseen
eye.
So, we lift our voices and cry,

Ohhhhh, oh, oh, oh! Ohhhhh, oh, oh, oh!
Ahhhhh, ah, ah, ah! Ahhhhh, ah, ah, ah!

We sing euphorically in the open night air, with the energy of every round going higher. Several congregants begin the dance of Shekem, jutting their shoulders, clapping their hands, and stomping their feet in sync, making love to the down beats. The bodies of those swaying float left and right like tall Lebanon cedars pushed around by strong desert winds. After a while, Dawit slows the rhythm, and the vigor of the crowd decelerates accordingly. The transition invites some people to sit back down on mats and cushions, and Dawit begins a solo.

You use my heart to exploit my loyalty,
Like a swine of a groom who erases her identity,
Like the plagues of Misra'yim we saw in Alke-bulan,

Like the thorny Jujube's torment of a lover's hand.
Why do you oppress me thus?
Son of Kish who comes for me, to make me sleep in the
dust.
But like the priest of Lamar, I will redirect my point of
view,
Simply piercing the facts to see Yahu.

I free me to reimagine the wrong.
I free me to move up and on.
I free me to sing a victory song.
The Yahu in me, the free.

Skip hell altogether, look into soul's validity.
Where the perfect law is, Yahu's law of liberty.
Radiating spiritually at will and reaping their own.
As a man thinks, so is he known.
I am strong, never again weak.
Rich, no poverty can speak.
Not by fate, by weapons, nor multitude of crew
Simply piercing the facts to see Yahu.

I free me to reimagine the wrong.
I free me to move up and on.
I free me to sing a victory song.
The Yahu in me, the free.

Perfect liberty is left not to things coming raw.
It draws my expected future in peace; I am in awe.
Heart with mind is soul, man's creative engine.
One, in the image of Yahu; simply call it an extension,
Or the kingdom of heaven within.
From where tomorrow begins.

Being first high priest like Aharon back then.
Yosef and Yahoshea dipping in.
Embolden by the energy therein.
No worries about when.
No care about what's been.
No missing the mark, which I call sin.
Redefining the notion of win.
Truth is basically akin.
Good news for all who need to recreate again and
again,
Through Yahu's liberating justice: love. Love
reigns.

I free me to reimagine the wrong.
I free me to move up and on.
I free me to sing a victory song.
The Yahu in me, the free.
I won't be small in my own mind.
I won't be small in my own mind.
I won't be small in my own mind.

The music fades as Dah's strumming ends. Many in the crowd whoop and clap, appreciating the sermon in song. Others sit still, tears streaming down their faces. Few seem aware of or bothered by the depth of the night, not too far from morning twilight. We're already in day two of Dah's visit.

Even after the cock crows, I awake slowly and slumber

in bed, blinded for a moment by midmorning sun rays reflecting off my brass wash basin. The quiet of the compound suggests others are also having a slower-than-usual start to this day. After checking the animal stall, I stroll toward the food house where people are moving about and helping themselves to baskets and jars filled with nourishment from the night's new moon feast. And talking. A lot.

"Last night was electric."

"Can you believe how he's being hunted down by, well, you know who?"

"I would've thought he'd be much bigger, kind of like that giant he took down."

"Did you hear how he played the lyre?"

"Think what it must have been like between him and his wife, the king's own daughter, when he escaped out the window."

"I wonder how long he'll be here."

"The king may be coming here too."

"Where will he go next?"

And on and on. I suspect that Dawit will be the topic of conversations all day, though he's not anywhere around the food house. I find him in the back courtyard under the shade of a lattice canopy with his crew. They are heavy into Abar, a two-person game where a player's six pawns pass across three rows of ten squares on a board. I watch for a while with a couple of other spectators.

Dah and Kurib take turns tossing five wooden coins to determine how many spaces to advance their pawns, sometimes jumping over or swapping places with the rival's pawns. Opponents can bump unprotected pawns back to an earlier square or force it into quicksand or some other rewarding, restricting, or penalizing place. Players also have three divinity stones that they pulled from a small, woolen pouch prior to the game's start which they can use to reap an advantage. We onlookers *ooh* and *aah* at the back-and-forth shuffle. Kurib steadily thumps his temple with his index finger, contemplating the best tactic from his toss. Dah's last coin toss was without a useful move, so he passes. When Kurib lays down a divinity stone, he sends Dah's last pawn back to the beginning square, walks his own last pawn off the board, and wins the game. The rest of us clap our appreciation, then Raddai and Ozem excitedly start a new game. I decide to visit Uzi.

"*Tweeeeet-tweeeeet-kola.*" I'm getting it. Kind of.

Uzi steadily looks out of his narrow stall window though his ears turn toward me.

"Hey," I say softly, rubbing his head. "I came to check your feed and that you are well. How is my new best friend?"

He turns his head and taps my shoulder with his nose.

"I hope to soon take you to the mountain pastures so you may roam freer and search for food that pleases and benefits you. I think it could help stimulate your mind and strengthen your body." He widens his eyes slightly. "Curious? Good." *I think we may be bonding.*

"Who are you talking to?" Dah's voice makes me jump.

"Woah, you surprised me."

"I didn't mean to. You good?"

"Yes, I'm fine, but it's wise to not slip up on people and animals. A grown man could get hurt, you know."

"I heard you speaking but didn't see anyone."

"You don't see Uzi?"

"The horse-mule?"

"Yes. I was talking to him if that's okay."

"Whatever makes you happy, my love." He moves closer and puts his hand on the small of my back.

"This animal is looking much better, even since the two days that I've been here."

"I think so too." I rub Uzi's head again. "The exercise, feed, fresh air, and tender care are doing him good."

"That would do anyone some good. How do I get some of that?"

Before I can answer, shouting erupts from behind the south storeroom where the game of Abar was taking place. We hurry back to hear Raddai and Ozem in a lively debate.

"Hold on, brothers, hold on," Dawit interrupts after a quick listen. "Rad, you say that the battle at Yeriychow is the most notable victory in Eber Y'israelite history because of the faith of our people to obey Yahu in the meekest orders resulted in the emphatic crumble of the city walls and our taking the city." Raddai nods as Dah turns to my brother. "Abiyah, you say that it was our win at Ay where we shrewdly used a large group of warriors to draw the enemy's army away from the city so that a smaller group could then go into the city to raid and wreck it."

"Exactly," Abiyah replies.

"Then, O, you say that it was a midnight ploy by Gideon's small forces to defeat the large Midianite army. And I could argue that it was the fight at Elah valley when a young, handsome Ebre lad conquered the P'lishtim giant with his sling and delivered the enemy's head to the king, but then I might be biased." He pauses as we absorb his jolly swagger with our own glee.

"Given our many amazing triumphs by the hand of Yahu, there is no end to this nonsensical dispute. So, let's say you fellas conclude the matter in a way that mocks—or dare I say slays—your apparent boredom: with a foot race." People standing nearby burst into cheers.

"A foot race wouldn't be fair to O and Abiyah, would

it?" Raddai quips. "I mean, this one has more girth than I and this one is, well, old." He refers to Ozem and Abiyah respectively.

"That may be true, my flawless, righteous, older Rad, but don't deceive yourself." Ozem is as much a jokester as his brothers. "My one stride equals two of yours."

"And I may be older than you two, but I'm just as strong—strong enough to embarrass both of you," Abiyah adds, exciting the bystanders even more. I start praying for him.

The last time we had such play in Ramah was twelve moons ago when Tiye announced a contest to celebrate the one who could eat the most of her much-loved lentil stew. I think she was trying to cook away the surplus of lentils in the storeroom. The event lasted one hour after the winner, a young priest trainee, gobbled down eleven big bowls. He threw up shortly after that.

Here, running can be treacherous. Even with the high physical prowess our people are known for, consider what a scorching sun, hot dry air, bare slopes, and rocky paths can do to a body in a dynamic, forward-propelling motion. Yet, our determined competitors, who have already shed their tunics or tucked them into their sashes, seem eager to do it.

The sun is low in the western sky, which should lighten the air and breathing conditions. As soon as deputy Noach announces a proper race route—out the front gatehouse, left along the outer wall, down the northwest hill for about a mile, pass the waterless well of Binah, right turn around the old, crooked olive tree that stands alone, and return—more folks start assembling along the course with their makeshift flags and cooling drinks in hand.

Abbah is at the front gate in time to call the three athletes to the starting line and commence the race.

"Gentlemen, run well and always run to win," he says. "Ready? Go!"

The runners take off, kicking up dust and snorting as much air as their lungs can hold as they dash over sand ridges and rocky slopes. The intensity of the sideline cheers tells us that the runners are advancing and hints to where they might be. In about twenty minutes, Ozem breaks the sunset's yellow-orange hilltop, trotting up toward us and crossing the finish line to great shouts, applause, and pats on the back. He's followed shortly by Raddai and, a little while more, Abiyah. O loftily credits the win to his youth, sturdily built body, skills, and grit. All three men huff and puff their way back through the gate, chugging melon water. *Mighty warriors,* I think and giggle, *who could use some endurance training. The champion too.*

We disperse to make ourselves ready for evening meal and I check once more on the animals, calling out our signal to Uzi. Nothing. He is dozing peacefully on a bed of hay. The water bowls and food troughs are all topped off for the night.

The girl in my mirror is pleased before I go to the inner court where the meal setting is as charmingly inviting as it was for the new moon last night. Abbah prays over the bulk of Ramah who are gathered, inducing gratitude to Yahu and love for one another.

"Halal Yahu," we all say together, concluding the invocation.

"For one more night, let us eat, drink, and be merry together," Abbah commands joyously. "This day's sun will see us go to Naioth."

Go? Who? Why? I knew it was coming. I knew it.

CHAPTER 6

BELIEF

*[be-lēf]: an acceptance that a
statement is true or that something exists.*

THE NEWS, THOUGH NOT TOO SURPRISING, tempers my craving for tonight's savory barley and chickpea stew, garlicky leeks, coriander cabbage, and honey bread. I end up sitting on the ledge of the western inner wall, opposite the feasters, to have a private meal of bread and sweet milk.

The thin crescent moon floats above an assembly of silhouetted ridgelines and trees behind the village—silent observers who, no doubt, are laughing at the foolish girl sitting alone on a clear blue night, grieving the absence of an unexpected belove who hasn't even departed her presence, yet. *Foolish girl who is already betrothed. Longing for one she cannot have.*

"May I intrude on your private party?" It's Dah behind me, having figured out my maze of camouflaged stones jutting vaguely from the wall and leading up to my high roost.

"What did I just tell you about slipping up on people?"

"My apologies, queen. Please forgive my blunder and allow me into your pleasing presence."

He finds a way to delight me and make me smile. "You may, since you did find me."

"It wasn't hard," he says, sitting down beside me and playfully bumping my arm. "I just followed the smoke coming out of your nostrils and when I found you, I had Ozem throw me up as high as he could. I grabbed a stone and crawled my way to the top. See? My hands are raw from the ragged edges."

"Stop teasing, silly," I simper and bump him right back.

"I saw how you walked off after Shmuel announced that we were leaving tomorrow and thought it best to give you some space. That bothered you?"

"No," I lie and hope it's undetected. "I thought I would enjoy some soli—"

"I can't stay here, Aby," Dah cuts in. "It's too dangerous for you and Zellah and all the others. Shmuel and I are pretty sure that Shaul will come this way soon. I'd rather he looks for me in Naioth, a more isolated place for me to insulate and plan my response to his irrational chase. Trust me, if I could safely stay and be with you, then I would. But I care too much for you to put you in harm's way."

"Have you not seen the might of my sling?" I try to lighten the mood. "I can handle myself."

"Yeah, and despite the fact that your sling still needs all the expertise I can give it, I still must go." We chuckle again. "I'll be back when things die down. Until then, you can see me anytime you want and I can see you . . . in the sky."

"The sky?"

"Yes. Lie back." He gently guides my shoulders and head down onto the bumpy stone, then lies on his back. The top of his head touches the top of mine. "Look."

The upper heaven opens its stage. Distant stars of pastel blue, yellow, white, and pink hues warm up and begin to dance. Some flicker in and out of view. Others, like so-called strange women of the night, present their seductive brilliance boldly and non-stop. Then others seem to fall rapidly from their resting places, sending luminous tracks of light running across the sky as if they are performing before a spellbound audience.

"Splendor," I whisper slowly, careful not to disturb the firmaments before me. "Amazing signs in the sky."

"There. Over there." He takes my hand and points it to a group of seven bright and familiar stars that congregate among some fourteen others. "See those?"

"Un-huh," I answer. "Ayish."

"The great bear," we say simultaneously.

"That's you," Dah says.

"I'm the bear?"

"Yes. Like her up in the heavens, you are the strongest, bravest, gentlest, fieriest, and loveliest female to wander our land, leading us all to freedom." He pauses to let that sink in. "A little farther down to the left is an even brighter star." He guides my finger toward it. "You see it?"

"Yes."

"That's Ash. That's me, the bear keeper who watches over you, the bear."

"My very own giant, reddish, beneficent guard?"

"Of course. I am right there . . ." he points to his star again, "whenever you need me."

"My Ash. I like that." I also like that he keeps holding my hand as we continue in awe of the heavens. "Do you believe Yahu is up there?"

"Up there and everywhere."

"Hmm. Even in the evils down here, especially to the innocents?"

"Yes, in a way."

"What way?"

"In that Yahu is in all, through all, and as all. And, thus, we create the same way that Yahu does. We think, we choose, we create, whether it be for good or for evil, even to the innocents or even our own selves, at least, that's what Shmuel tells me. The choice of what we produce is ours to make in every moment of every day."

"Choices," I murmur, considering the big one I made for my betrothal.

"You haven't yet made the choice to be a wife, though I'm sure that you have had many offers," Dah says. "Why is that?"

My stomach twists at his inquiry. "There have been inquiries, but a husband? I don't think so."

"No?" Dah's reaction is conventional.

"It's that I have another intent that may not adapt so well to being the chattel of another, though I would hope that that would not be the case, but you never know."

"An intent like what?"

"Like the abandoned and abused children that I mentioned yesterday or, you know, other heroic stuff to save the world." We laugh, once more, at my lighthearted diversion.

"Anything is possible if you believe that it is," he replies.

"What is it like being married?"

"I'm pretty sure I'm not married now, but when I was, it was fine right up until her father tried to kill me. I doubt that it was like most Eber Y'israelite marriages." His voice trails off a little. "She was the king's daughter. We lived in the king's palace, under his nose. But we had affection for and connection with one another in a wonderful way. At least, I think so."

"You miss her."

"I do and think often of peace for her. You're here, though, and that's a joy that I didn't expect." His tone is back to being playful. "Let's make a pact. If I survive Shaul's pursuit, then I'll come back here, and you and I will be married. Deal?"

"Deal." *I wish I could. I hope that I can. Belief must preserve me.*

The next morning, after another good night's sleep and cultivation time with Yahu, I walk out into a mauve dawn to greet the faint crescent moon and its few still-visible companions. Perhaps, they can do something celestial to delay the departure of my father and my friend. I hurry through my chores, getting at last to Uzi.

"*Tweeeeet-tweeeeet-kola-kola-tweet-tweet-kola-tweeeeet.*" I start his grooming and he lets out a slow sigh, indicating bliss from the skin massage. "This is Dah's last day here and maybe my last chance to tell him how I feel."

"*Tweeeeet-tweeeeet-kola-kola-tweet-tweet-kola-tweeeeet,*" Uzi sounds out and nudges me to a stall below his.

"His donkey is gone?" I ask, and Uzi nods.

"With Dawit?"

Uzi nods.

"But where?"

Uzi raises his head high and pretends to chew.

"Gan Aby."

Uzi nods profusely.

I leave to satisfy the girl in the mirror before Uzi and I head southeast.

Before we arrive in Gan Aby, Dawit is already there, sitting on his knees cushioned by a multicolored wool blanket. Hands on his knees. Eyes closed, guarded by long lashes and thick brows. Lips relaxed together. Locs cascading to his chest. Chin tilted to the sky, showing his thin, finely shaped mustache and close-cut beard. Smoke rises from a small, round heap of burnt cannabis and frankincense resin, smoldering on a nearby rock and lifting the garden's earthy and fruity aroma. Dah, my Ash, is in the stillness.

I get down from Uzi, walk quietly into Gan Aby, and wait. And watch his serenity. The balanced curves of his face—wide and flat forehead, round nose, high cheeks, square chin—glisten like copper under a summer sun. Though I wonder what tension might be brewing in his mind. The man we call our anointed king, the one for whom Dawit has fought for, consoled, and protected loyally, wants him dead. He is a refugee in his own home.

"Aby?" Dawit asks, ending my contemplation. "Had I known you were here, I would have hastened my meditation."

"No, there's nothing more important than the stillness, seeing yourself, and knowing Yahu."

"Indeed. I'm glad we agree." He stands to stretch his legs.

"But is it safe for you to do that out here alone when Shaul is hunting you?"

"I think so. You're concerned?"

"Well, I'd hate for your body to get snatched on earth while the rest of you is in heaven," I giggle. "You could at least have a companion to watch."

"I'm fine. Besides, Yahu has my front, back, and sides." He turns completely around, smiling. I smile, too, enjoying the view.

"Why don't you just kill him?" The question is thick, but I am unafraid to ask it.

"Kill who?"

"Melek Shaul."

"Girl, don't be as mad-minded as he is, thinking with your flesh."

"How is that madness? Shaul no longer follows the instruction of Yahu and is now tormenting his own court for no reason. Doesn't our law say to cut down such evil? To rid ourselves of the things and people that corrupt us; people that—how did Abbah put it? Oh yeah—'bring on ourselves the curses of the law'?"

"Well, first, I appreciate that you were listening. And secondly, peace, woman, peace. I swear you can get real worked up in no time at all."

"You killed the giant, the lion, and the bear."

"That was different. They were all responses to attacks."

"Exactly, and that's what Shaul is doing. He's attacking you and basically his own people."

Dah seems to ponder the thought for some odd reason. *There's nothing to ponder.*

"There is truth to that. But, Aby, we are more than human. We are spirit first which means that Shaul is still a son of Yahu and our brother. He was picked to be our king, even if reluctantly so. It's not up to me to decide what to do about him."

"Well, killing him would end your running and you wouldn't have to leave Ramah."

"I'm not running because I'm afraid of being killed by Shaul. I'm running to keep me from killing him, which I could easily do. But I made an oath before Yahu to serve the chosen king, and I aim to keep it. How 'bout we change the subject?" The fret washing across his deep brown eyes confirms that he's had enough talk about killing.

"I hear that many Ebres call you the lion of Y'hudah," I say. "A beast with fearless speed and unyielding in battle."

"Yeah, that's funny. I hear it, too, sometimes."

"Emah says they mean your conviction and might. Just this much shy of Yahu's." I make a smidgen of a pinch with my fingers.

"Nope, not at all. I'm just a shepherd boy who loves sheep; a boy fully confident in having Yahu within him."

"Yahu within, huh? You and Yahu together."

"There's no other way for me."

"I can feel that truth," I say after thinking about it for a moment. "Yahu within me, and we are one together. I always thought so but was mainly taught to live by Moshe's law. To see Yahu as out there somewhere, far beyond me."

"Herding sheep alone in the desert gives you a lot of time to learn about Yahu and there's much more to know than what's in the law. Don't get it sideways, though; I love the purpose of the law to normalize outward behaviors and procedures even if with fear and limited effect. But learning to be as one with Yahu is a heart thing, an inner work thing. Law does not regulate the heart."

"We sure act like it does. Maybe from my beginnings or from Abbah and Emah, I've always felt in my heart that I can do anything and be anything, if I believe I can with Yahu's help. If I don't, then I won't, right?" He nods. "So, Yahu and law seem in conflict."

"No, not really. Moshe's law came from Yahu, so it, in its pureness, cannot be in conflict. The conflict comes from how we see it. Many of our people embrace strange interpretations of the law that then bear strange fruit, like Shaul's dowry of P'lishtim foreskins for his daughter or our keeping foreigners as slaves when our own people hated their enslavement when they were foreigners in Misra'yim or obligatory giving to Yahu or—"

"Abusing children for vanity's sake. I get it."

"Yeah . . . okay then . . . well . . . you can see how the imperfect and frail shrink the intent of the unlimited."

"It can make it very hard to follow and to know what to do."

"Sure, if you aim to please the interpreters rather than the originator. Go straight to the originator for both the understanding and your correspondingly next action."

"Un-huh."

He leans back and laughs. "And if you must await any delayed answers," he pulls out his lyre and starts to play, "then let meaningful music lift you up."

We sing and dance around Gan Aby, letting rhythms take our good mood even higher until we bump into each other, collapse on green grass, and roll together onto a bed of purple and blue irises. I land on top and instantly the magnet that is him pulls in the metal that is me. I see it in his eyes and, undoubtedly, he sees it in mine. We know we shouldn't, but we do. He raises his head to mine. I inhale the slightest whiff of his sweetness, perfumed with his own brand of frankincense, myrrh, and masculinity. Our lips touch gracefully, like feathers landing on still water. I close my eyes to better feel what is happening. The caress is curiously delicious and quickly blooms into a warm and fiery fusion that conveys his passion and sends the now familiar spark rushing down my spine. His fingers weave under my headwrap and clench my head, loosening a few of my curls to sweep his cheek. His manhood announces his elation. Our embrace eases, then lingers before ending. My heart pulsates so hard that he must feel it pounding his chest. We look into each other's eyes without speaking, seeking a favorable reception, I think. He holds my cheeks in his hands.

"Are you okay?" he whispers.

"I am," I whisper back without moving. "Are you? I mean, did you break a vow or something?"

"No," he chuckles. "I'm fine, too, but do forgive me if I offended you in any way."

"You didn't. We didn't."

"For obvious reasons, though, we should keep this just between us."

"Agreed." *Absolutely so.* I roll over onto my back to lie next to him.

"Aby . . ." he says, raising up on his left elbow to look at me. "I appreciate these last three days with you. They have been enlightening and delightful, and it means a lot to me. You mean a lot to me. I love you, so always know that."

"I feel the same but know that there are more pressing matters at hand right now than the two of us." Exhilaration and sadness fill me at once. I love him, too, but can't do anything about it. "It'll all work out for our good, right, my Ash?"

"Yes, my Ayish, and I will return for you. Only you."

He kisses my hand and holds onto it. We lie still for a while, absorbing the calm and the colorful, fragrant beauty of Gan Aby. How I wish for this to never end but know that it must. I can only hope to be with him like this again one day. Soon.

About an hour after we return to Ramah, Abbah and Dah are ready to leave for Naioth, where most of the priests and priest trainees live. Noach, Raddai, Ozem, and Kurib are going with them. They will plan matters of security, for Dah and for the Eber Y'israelite nation. I knock on the wall outside of Abbah's office and he invites me in.

"Abbah, you ready to go?"

"Yes, my Abyga'el, I'm ready." He smiles and opens his arms to me, flashing his own warm, brown eyes surrounded by firm, glowing skin, and bushy black-and-gray brows. His hug is luscious and comforting. I feel grateful. I have my Abbah back, despite the shock and disappointment I brought upon him. I hope that I can regain his trust somehow, somewhere. "I may not get back before you leave to . . . for . . . Ma'on."

"But, Abb—" He raises an index finger, stopping my rebuttal.

"All is well." He pauses to sigh. "I have comfort from Yahu that, though you may shoulder some burden, this betrothal shall end favorably for you. I do not know how and that's not of interest to me at this point, but it will be for good and not evil. As such, I will not seek to contest it, despite my disapproval of what you did and how you went about doing it. You will eat that fruit, however bitter or sweet it may be." Abbah hugs me tight in silence for a moment, then pushes me back.

"In a few days, a representative from Nabal will come for you. If I don't make it back before you leave, then know that I'll join you there in time for the ceremony. You are my daughter and I bless you. I will always act for your highest good. I also know that your mother and I taught you the very best that we could for you to know what you want in this life, know what produces good, believe in it, make wise choices toward it, and trust in Yahu's power to bring them to their fullness."

"I know, Abbah. You've told me that many times."

"I have, but I need for it to stick here," he points to my temple. "And here," he points to my heart. "Emah has my instructions and knows what to do to send you off as you should go and with enough time to prepare. She will appoint a handmaiden to go with you to attend to your needs. You're leaving my house, but not my heart. You are welcome wherever I am. And, Aby, please guard your agreements with more vigor. It pains me to think of your being hitched to an errant thought, something you don't want to experience, even for a moment. What's done is done but let us put our belief only on the virtue or praise to come from it," he touches my heart and my forehead, "until it materializes."

"Yes, Abbah, I understand. I will think on the children and on you and Emah. Of all the things that I will miss about this place . . ." I say, looking around his office. Warm. Nurturing. Loving. Home. I turn back toward him. "I will miss you most."

"I love you." We embrace again.

"Is love enough, Abbah?"

"Love for Yahu, for yourself, and then equally for others is always enough . . . for anything."

I help him with the last of his things and we walk to the outer court where the others are waiting.

"You ready, old man?" Dawit asks. They load up their mules, say their goodbyes, and head out. Despite my belief, I am left betwixt: my body will be in Ma'on but my mind and heart will be with my Ash.

CHAPTER 7

BEKNOWN

[be-nown]: to know someone or something.

WHAT FEELS LIKE A FULL LUNAR cycle has only been seven days since Abbah and Dah left. Every night I fall asleep dreaming of when Dah and I were last in Gan Aby and awake each day with a fast-beating heart and a smile on my face.

This morning, that smile first greets Emah, who is in the garden behind our house next to her herb shed, drying plants that she uses to help ease people's physical and mental infirmities.

"You're up later than usual today," she says. "Slept well, I hope?"

"I did, Emah. Uzi and I roamed the northwest lands yesterday looking for throw-aways. We didn't find any, so I left some of my ribbons with a few healers of the towns."

"That's a good thing, right?"

"It is. I saw a few children who looked thin and nervous, but they were with adults, so we moved on."

"You're getting pretty attached to that mule, huh?"

"He's special, unlike other animals I've known. I think we make a good team."

"Good. Right now, I need you to team up with me on these herbs."

She calls out a batch of orders and I go about separating, bunching up, and tying together stems of purple hyssop flowers, white coriander flowers, and green dill leaves. I hang the bunches upside down under a screened shed in the warm air where they'll dry out over the next few weeks. I then lay caraway fruit, black cumin seed pods, and cinnamon peels on flat clay boards inside a long, screened shelf outside the shed to roast gently in the sun.

I am finishing up my noon meal when the ram's horn blows. *An approaching visitor. Probably the one we expect. The legate from Nabal. Coming for me.*

At the main gate, I fade into the crowd already gathering there. We gawk at our latest visitor as he glides down the wide, wooden steps of a long, lofty wagon drawn by two big horses and covered with bright purple linen trimmed in gold ribbon.

"Greetings to all and all praises be to Allah, the one whom you refer to as Yahu, given that there is only one Creator God, and that one favored me to be in your presence today."

The man stands and speaks majestically from the last step of the wagon. The energy around us pulsates joy with every word that jumps from his lips.

"I am Mohinder Charkravarti Mahawar, so named by my grandfather, may he sit happily among the ancestors, that I should be a superior guard of things skyward and highly valued which I have come here to do. Being the beloved people and friends that I am certain you are, I beg you to simply call me Moh."

Long legs of the tall man step boisterously onto the

courtyard. He looks around slowly and cautiously at his awaiting audience as if he's documenting each of our faces even as we evaluate his chestnut cheeks, smooth and round like the nut itself, shimmering in the midafternoon sun. Mirroring his regal stance is his attire: shiny soft-blue tunic trimmed along the neck, front, knee-length helm, and sleeves in a bright gold tapestry. Matching blue pants cling to his lower legs, ending at flat, gold tapestry shoes. A wide, dark blue, velvety corset sash wraps around the man's narrow waist, highlighting his broad chest. From the sash, a left-side-front tail, also trimmed in the same gold tapestry, hangs to his knees. A brown leather belt with a silver buckle sits atop the sash while a thinner sash made of the gold tapestry crosses his body from his right shoulder to his left hip. Gold, blue, and white beads decorate his neck and gold rings adorn his ears and fingers. His hands rest upon the handle of a long, curved, silver filigree sword—glistening with sapphire stones—that touches the ground delicately. Completing his attire is a blue and gold turban with a gold and silver brooch center front and a white ornamental feather that rises over its top. *It's a lot to take in at once.*

"Let it beknown," Moh continues, "that I salute you as the humble and reliable servant of his lord, Nabal, of the house of Kalebtu in Ma'on. I am here to call upon his holiness, lord Shmuel, the high priest and elder of the Ebre Y'israelite nation."

"Welcome to Ramah," Emah greets, already at the front of the crowd with her arms extended toward the humble and reliable servant. "I am Zellah, wife of Shmuel, who is away regrettably on an obligation and who has entrusted your care to me. We have awaited your advent with great anticipation and open our home to you and yours."

"Oh splendid, Madam Zellah!" Moh bows to Emah, kissing her hand. "I am delighted to meet you despite the absence of his holiness. As you know, the bridal price for the most precious one, Abyga'el, daughter of lord Shmuel, was fulfilled seven days ago. Lord Nabal's betrothal obligations to his holiness and your honorable family are, therefore, complete. My task as his servant, simply for clarification, is to escort the virtuous bride safely to Ma'on where the betrothal agreement will conclude in praise and celebration as it is written and expected."

"Of course," Emah confirms. "Come, refresh yourselves, and prepare to enjoy our community's evening meal. We will discuss any open details afterward. Please."

Emah gestures to five student priests who unload the wagon and show Moh and his two attendants to their dwelling place. She sends a messenger to Nabal at Kalebtu in Ma'on to acknowledge Moh's arrival and confirm my entrance there as his bride a week after the next new moon. Thirty days.

Chef Tiye presents another scrumptiously diverse feast and Ramah celebrates our newcomers with foot washing, dancing, and merriment well into the night. When morning comes, I roll up my wool pallet bed, change my clothes, sit in stillness, and depart to start my day. As I step out, Moh jumps up from his seat on the floor and bows his head.

"Aah!" *What the—*

"My apologies, my lady, Abyga'el. I did not mean to frighten you."

Unlike yesterday's embellished guise, Moh wears a murky purple, loose-fitting tunic with buttons from the waist up. Beneath it are matching loose trousers. He looks much more comfortable without the weight of the formal turban, freeing his dark, shoulder-length rumpled hair to frame his flaxen eyes, thick but shapely brows, and square chin. His look invites a warm connection.

"What are you doing here?" I await what I hope is a glorious explanation.

"My duty."

"Your duty?"

"Yes. It is my job to see to and protect you."

"First off, it's just Aby, not Abyga'el, and certainly not 'my lady.' Secondly, I can see to and protect myself, thank you very much. There's no need for you to do that, especially in Ramah."

"I understand and certainly appreciate your assessment, however, it is my charge, and I am not one to neglect my responsibilities."

He must be kidding. I shrug my shoulders, pull together my headscarf, and walk outside toward the meal house to start my chores. Moh follows me like a lamb after its mother. I stop and turn around.

"What? What now?"

"Nothing."

"Why are you following me?"

"As I stated earlier, it is my charge. I am here to watch over and serve you. It is not my intent to be a bother."

I scan his posture and consider his convincing sincerity, then concede. "Come on."

We go through my tasks, ending with animal care.

"I remember him," Moh says, pointing to Uzi. "It's been a while since I've seen him though."

"Allow me to reacquaint you. Moh, this is Uziyah. Uziyah, this is Moh." Uzi nods to the almost stranger.

"Uziyah?" Moh says slowly, inspecting Uzi and patting his back.

"Uzi for short." I start my brushing routine.

"I don't recall that he had a name when he was in Kalebtu." Moh stops speaking to wave away and spit out feather-like wisps of horse-mule hair floating into his face. "Nor do I remember him being this feeble."

"He was worse than this when Nabal delivered him here. Matted hair. Sunken eyes. Jutting ribs. Sad and infuriating. Like he had been tortured."

"With intent, I'm sure."

"What do you mean?" My jaw tightens. *With intent.*

"Such a presentation is typical of Massa, se—"

"Massa?" The tight jaw starts to lock.

"That's what I call him, considering that he is a burden to me and most everyone else. He sent you what he sees as a lavish yet comedic message. Basically, that he alone is lord—at least, in Kalebtu—who determines the state of even the finest things. Like you. If I remember correctly, Uzi was taken from Kalebtu about two months before coming here. To where, I don't know."

A Massa indeed. "It doesn't matter. He's mine now and I give him special attention every day so that he can be at his best. I named him Uzi so that he always knows that Yahu is his strength."

"You think he would ever know that?"

"For sure." I wink at Uzi and I think he winks back. "He is smart and very special."

Moh leans against a beam, pointing out any flaws in my grooming method and adding insightful commentary here and there. He says that Massa bred Uzi from a stallion father and a donkey mother. Most mules come from donkey fathers and horse mothers. That's why Uzi looks and acts more like a horse than a donkey with his shorter ears, stronger legs, rounder hooves, and swifter gait. His kind appears more intelligent than horses and more cooperative than donkeys, and his white coat supposedly implies a high social rank of its owner. Due to genetics, reproducing the breed is fickle and risky, and when it does occur, the offspring are born sterile. Still, Massa is hell-bent on doing it because he can—and to confirm his own self-declared genius. *A Massa indeed.*

"Other than fetch his betroths, what do you do for Nabal?"

"Consider me the palace steward, bestowed with collecting, protecting, and growing the value of Massa's most prized possession: his livestock, which to him includes his money and his wives."

"And how many wives might that be?"

"You would make four."

Only four? I had hoped for more so that he would touch my body as little as possible. "And concubines?"

"Yes."

Good. I relax some. "In your role, you would also work for me?"

"Not really, but sometimes, depending on Massa's wishes."

"That's good to know." We finish with Uzi and walk to the meal house. "You're not from Kanaan."

"Wow. You're extraordinarily perceptive."

"I'll take that little quip as a compliment, thank you. So, where are you from, and how did you get here?"

Moh answers while we eat. He was nine when his family relocated from Bharat, a land far east of Kanaan, to Alkebu-lan. Moh's father, Rishyasringa Marawar, had been invited to teach natural holistic medicine at the Per-Ankh, a school of higher learning in Misra'yim. The government of southern Bharat granted him and his family—Moh, his sister, and his mother—paperwork to travel. Moh's mother could not have been more delighted and hopeful. She had long awaited to escape the exclusion and oppression that Bharatans inflicted on one another based on complexion-driven social castes—preference for lighter skin citizens and bias against darker ones, more strange fruit of standards implanted years ago by emphatic, pale-skinned settlers for their own benefit. Indigenous people there, who now idolize ashen skin, are both victim and oppressor.

It was a group of Bharatan priests who brutally attacked Moh's swarthy, cocoa-skinned grandfather for having crossed the doorstep of a light-skin-only office building to keep an elderly woman from falling on her face onto the street. It was prohibited for him to do so. The priests almost killed him.

"That's insane . . ." I blurt out, stunned by the illogic. Judging people by their skin? Here, skin is skin. It's the outer container, like the casing on a grape or an olive. It may show texture differences, even bruises, but it simply contains the inside where the true person resides. What Shaul is doing to Dawit, for example, is coming from within his heart and mind, not from his skin.

"On that, we certainly agree and—"

"Besides, the original human had dirt-brown skin . . ." I rant on, recalling that Eber Y'israelites have been a mixed people for a long time, both kin and strangers, of tribes who followed the ways of Yahu, rather than being a people of a certain color or blood. We are varied shades of rich earthy tan, brown, and burnt tones, so much so that no one even notices skin. Or hair texture. Or any such petty features.

I think of the story of our ancestor Myriam. Her coffee-colored hand once suddenly turned white as a reprimand from Yahu for her jealousy and rebellion, frightening those around who all saw it as a sign of disgrace and death rather than privilege and status. "And dark came before light, the evening before the day. In darkness, the universe was born and in darkness, we continue to create. And-and-and skin complexion is involuntary. No one chooses the physical features they're born with."

"My goodness. Unwind yourself, would you?" Moh cautions as he glances at the other diners and nods pleasantly to them, making his bushy and luscious soot-black hair bounce back and forth on his shoulders. "What you say is true, still such bias is what happened to my family and what continues to happen in my homeland, so—"

"But what keeps it going?"

"All right... well... basically, it's the continual agreement with the reimagined standard, either by force or by need or by choice, which then informs everything else."

"Explain."

"A stronger force of people redefines a society's values to their likeness. Want of advantages, like privilege, or fear of disadvantages, like subjugation, drives acceptance by the masses. And so, it is."

"Sounds like wickedness to me and I'm glad that I don't know it." Sure, my ancestors were first immigrants and then slaves in Misra'yim for more than four hundred years. The king of the Misra'yim, who looked like us, I'm told, feared our numbers, our know-how, and our god, so he used oppression as an offensive tool to guard the station of his people and his kingdom. We never saw ourselves as inferior to them and it certainly was not about body features. The reality of torture won out.

"I, too, am glad that you don't know it," Moh says. "It's a generational, deep-rooted disorder that is slow to change and, thus, no need for you to get so upset about it here and now. It produces nothing, so perhaps I may continue to answer your initial question of how I got here?"

"My apologies, please do."

And he does after we exit the meal house to get out of Tiye's way and find shady seats near the front gatehouse.

Moh and his family made their way to color-blind Alkebu-lan, stopping for a brief time in the south to visit a vibrant community of Bharatans and finally settling much farther up in On, a town in northeast Misra'yim near the college. The Marawars began to live a gratifying life, being treated with respect and encouraged to fully express their skills, intelligence, and creativity.

Moh especially excelled in languages, science, mathematics, reading, and writing. By the time he turned sixteen, he was an engineer apprentice, helping to develop the town's structure. He was organizing the building of a canal system to draw water from the lower Ye'or Iteru for irrigation when a band of Shasu nomads raided the city, taking away gold, cattle, and people, including Moh. They traded him to other nomads who eventually sold him to Nabal.

"That callous one had me castrated with silver clamps shortly after I arrived in Kalebtu, dedicating me to his gods and anointing me to keep watch over his wives and concubines."

My stomach gurgles at the thought before I can respond. "Are you okay?"

"Oh, yeah, I'm fine now. The sun didn't make me a eunuch in my mother's womb. Nor did I choose it on my own. Massa made me so without my consent, and I am turning his wickedness into my advantage."

"How so?"

"I'm fully determined in whatever I put my mind to, whether it's engineering a temple or guarding an assortment of women or grooming a special mule." Moh snickers and pats Uzi on the nose. "So, before too long, I began writing Nabal's messages to his associates, including the king, Shaul. I developed new techniques for sheep shearing, mediated better deals with wool buyers, and stood in for Massa in other business affairs. He was content to be relieved of it so that he could go explore other worlds with his friends. He privately calls me the confidential confidant of Kalebtu."

Moh and I continue like this for nearly three weeks, speaking easily during chores and over meals. Since he stopped sleeping outside of my quarters and following me around constantly, he's become quite the companion, advisor, and ally. When we're not together, I check in with him at least every third hour. So far, he has managed to catch up with me before I must honor that vow. His presence has been comforting, especially as my heart still aches for Dah.

We are in Gan Aby today, practicing our weaponry. I am focusing on extending the effective range of my slingshot. Moh is stepping cautiously as he speeds up the crisscross-patterned flail of his rod, a hard wooden stick about as round as a small cucumber and tall enough to reach his eyebrows. The air awakened by his practice motion makes the trees wobble and the flowers dance. We trade a few skill stories and tactics. Moh agrees to design and help me build a butterfly oasis in the garden. He goes further to suggest a better way to catch rainwater to help the plants flourish.

"Why are you doing this?" Moh asks unexpectedly, as we rearrange the rocks and stones to bring about his rain-water capture idea.

"Doing what?"

"Becoming wife to Nabal? You're obviously very

beautiful. Almost as lovely as I," he laughs. "And in just these fifteen days, I've found you to be strong, shrewd, and clever. Any man would pay as high a bride price as he could afford to take you as his wife. Rather than compatibility, you want opposition?"

"Opposition? What are you getting at?"

"I know Nabal as Massa because he is a burden and a hardship to me and others so I'm asking why you chose betrothal to him."

"I did not choose him because I needed him or anyone else to make me whole. I chose him because he had something the other suitors did not: large landholdings unconnected with the priesthood, particularly his forty-three acres in the Yarden valley."

He looks to the sky. "I'm familiar with it."

"Then you know that it is greeted in the front by water and protected in the back by mountains with mild valleys on either side. I saw it when I traveled down south with Abbah a little while ago and remember being struck by the beauty of its native shelter. It's a perfect spot for thrown-away children to be safe, well, and thrive. That was my bride price and why I am betrothed to Massa."

"A home for children who have no home," Moh says quietly, looking pleased and troubled at once. "Sounds like it may be worth it. I'm not sure, though."

"It is. About a third of children in Kanaan die by their fifth year, mostly due to them being sold, sacrificed, publicly stoned, neglected, or just cast aside," I paint a better picture for him.

"A short time ago, I came upon eleven-year-old Heziyah, shaken and huddled up behind a rock near Yebus, a city some five miles away from here. She was violated by her uncle, who wasn't much older than her, which resulted in pregnancy, so her mother tied her to a pole and let her brothers stone her, breaking her skin and hip bone. They then threw her out of the house for shaming the family. Before her, two sisters—Lelah and Tamar—who are just a bit younger than Heziyah, were about to be sold to satisfy family debts when they ran away from home and fell into starvation. I found ten-year-old boys, Yosiyah, and Kenan, tied to trees. Apparently, Yosiyah got sick with fever and to keep him from being a burden to them, his parents left him in a forest not far from where Kenan lived. When Kenan went hunting, he found Yosiyah and carried him to his father, who tied them up and whipped them for what he presumed was an inappropriate coupling. Kenan's father was happy to be rid of them and, frankly, I'm surprised they weren't killed. These are just a few of the many children I've found in the last nineteen moons."

"And such doings please your god?" Moh looks shocked.

"No. At least, not *my* god. Some adults claim that such treatment better trains and keeps a child from violating our laws. Others blame it on lack of food or some other harsh condition. I think it's more to satisfy their own evil interpretations and vile whims and few, if any, laws protect the children. The consequences for them almost breathing too hard are dreadful, primarily for those unlucky enough to be born a girl—the low-status gender that makes some weak fathers and mothers toss away their daughters."

"Surely you exaggerate."

"No, not really. Most folks just look the other way, content to tolerate the injustice as normal and move on. Not me."

"So, that's your life's mission, huh? To catch the little fallen stars on your broad shoulders?"

"Star catcher." I slap his back to lift the heaviness. "That's how I'll beknown."

CHAPTER 8

BESEECH

[be-sēCH]: ask someone
urgently and fervently to do something.

THE NEXT DAY AT FIRST MEAL, I am so entranced in
yet another conversation with Moh that I don't notice
Emah walking up behind me.

"Aby," Emah speaks, and I shriek. "I didn't mean to
startle you, dear. Still, I'm sure that Moh has had enough
talk of the sanctuary or your battles with the sling or whatever it is you're so fervent about." She chuckles and turns
to face my guardian. "Now, Moh, to what extent do your
escort duties go?"

"All the way to the heavens, if necessary."

"Excellent. I beseech you, then, to accompany us tomorrow. We will observe the new moon at Shoreshim in
the forest of Bashan."

Shoreshim. Forest of Bashan. A faraway place where my
aunts, Emah's sisters, Gullah and Ifrah, live. That's all I
know about it, other than Emah saying that there would
never be a need for me to go there.

"As you wish, Emah Zellah," Moh answers.

"Good. Let us prepare today to depart at sunrise."

Needs change, it seems, so I do as I'm told and ready myself and Uzi.

We head north at daybreak, passing along the east side of the bumpy-yet-grand Y'hudah hills, home to wild cattle grazing on pastures that grow greener and grassier as we move along. We stop every so often to shake off the soreness of our backsides, despite the thickness of the folded wool cloths between our butts and our animals' backs. Uzi's is especially a smooth ride. His gait is a constant, rhythmic cadence that cushions any jolt. A stop at one small village becomes the place of our first meal of pistachio nuts, olives, and bread. With satisfied bellies, we ride on. The sun starts to fall away and we soon arrive at the city of Tirtzah on the outskirts of the Eybal hills where we spread thick blankets on wide wooden platforms, joining other nearby travelers at an outdoor inn for sleeping.

Early the next morning, we continue north, soon greeted by the fruity scent of wild, white jasmine flowers that refresh the journey's air, if not its toil. We cross the Yarden and Yarmuk rivers where they join just below the soaring Bashan hills. Rocky boulders seem proud to prop up the rising pastures and high peaks weighed down by a forest abundant with lofty oaks, bushy nut and berry orchards, and wild flora in aromatic bloom—perching pads for an assortment of birds, butterflies, and bees. Large and little silvery patches scattered along the top of the bluish-gray mountain range cast a moon-like sheen to curious wildlife scurrying about. I stand there, gazing at the wonderment and rejecting the urge to lay prostrate before its splendor.

"White moonstone," Emah whispers, standing in reverence beside me. "Milky light from the moon's magic.

You'll have plenty of time later to be lost in its charm. We have a few more miles to go and I prefer that we get there before dark."

She nudges me along with her hands on my shoulders. We disappear into a thicket of bright, dark, and in-between green foliage, then drudge through the forest until we come to another kind of light—a radiant fire beetle or maybe a sliver of sunlight still left in the sky, simply floating among the trees.

"We're here." Emah stops.

"Where?" Moh and I say in unison.

Before she can answer, a door opens in front of us from nowhere, about four feet off the ground and between two trees. Two women run down six wide now-visible steps.

"Sistahhhhh," they scream and practically pull Emah off her donkey, hugging and kissing her. "You came! You came! We're so glad you're here!" They hug and kiss her some more.

"And this one," the younger woman exclaims, pointing a long finger at me. She is much younger than Emah, maybe twice my age. A clingy sash of teal and purple threads shows off her small waist and ample hips. Her toned arms tighten around my shoulders. "Can this be our darling Aby? The last time I saw you, you were just a little thing, playing in the dirt. Now look at you. Tall. Curvy. Beautifully bronzed. Just like me, your Dodah Ifrah." She bumps her hip against mine, almost knocking me over as she laughs heartily.

"And we hear that you've been a busy little something, getting all hitched up and without your father's knowledge," the older woman says, still holding onto Emah. She is my Dodah Gullah. Her frame is slightly larger than her sister's, noticeable even under a loose-fitting tunic.

"I love it," Ifrah shouts with slightly wild eyes beaming at me. "That's how to declare your feminine essence and free yourself to one day be legally equal to men. I love it."

"Come, everyone," Gullah takes over. "Let us settle you in."

"How is your house, uh, invisible?" I ask.

"That, my dear, is moonstone," Gullah answers. "Maybe you saw it on the mountain on your way here? We collected it, shaved it down, and covered our house with it. Its silvery sheen is like a mirror and reflects light, causing the house to magically disappear. After a few days, you'll get used to it. Come on."

The house is long and narrow, anchored outside upon many trees. Inside, large holes in the high ceiling covered by dried tree sap offer sky views without much risk of unwelcome elements getting in. Two oak trees run up through the wooden floor, helping to stabilize the structure and giving my aunts acorns to eat and more space to hang their many catchers, crystals, stones, and amulets. Large clay jars of oils, honey, water, and wine line a wall while hundreds of potted plants surround built-in benches and tables, emitting fresh aromas—the top of which is the sharp scent of shredded green grass from galbanum, Gullah's favorite. A door at the back of the house leads to outdoors where a hefty garden, surrounded by a tall fence of woven willow shoots, is home to more plants, a firepit, and a small gong. At the center of the garden is a tree. It stands about seven feet tall with seven branches at its top, but limbless toward its stout, smooth trunk. Its bark is painted white and carved with ornate drawings of lions and lilies from top to bottom. A wide band of woven water reeds encircles the tree.

"Moh?" I ask, as a tear plops down his face. "You okay?"

"I'm fine," he pauses, looking around. "This all reminds me of my grandmother. The garden. Herbs. Full jars. Rustic smell. It all reminds me of her kitchen back in Bharat years ago." He wipes his cheeks as we walk back to the middle of the house and rest on large, round cushions near the trees. Gullah and Ifrah flutter around with platters and bowls in the room closest to the front door before inviting us and those she calls "angels of Yahu" to gather at a long table to eat.

"My aunties," I turn to them in between bites. "Why do you live out here alone when there is plenty of room in Ramah with us?"

"I see our sister has been tight-mouthed about her family." Gullah rolls her eyes at Emah.

"Don't roll your eyes at me, Gul. I told her all she needed to know. Besides, Aby cares more about slinging stones than soaking saffron, okay?"

"Oh, a warrior princess, huh?" Ifrah jokes while Gullah raises her right hand high, the familiar hint for Ifrah to stop talking.

"Anyway, to answer your question, dear child," she continues. "West Bashan is our home. Literally, our roots are here, aren't they, Zellah? We stay in the forest because of legalistic, superstitious, and religious people who misunderstand who we are and what we do."

"Which is what?"

"We stir up the mysterious electric energy of plants and minerals into various, often more mysterious, inventions so that the fruit of earth satisfies the purposes for which they exist—medicinal, preservatory, protectionary, sensory, spiritual, religious, culinary, and mystical delights." *Huh?*

"You mean, like a witch doctor?" Moh asks. "That's what we call them in Bharat, my homeland."

"No," Ifrah answers with a sigh. "Being a witch could mean death here. More like a . . . a muse. A green muse."

"Oh, we were revered as mystics and spiritual advisors," Gullah says, looking back and forth between Moh and me. "People wanted it and most needed it. But they were taught by guardians of the law like your—"

"Gul," Emah is her stern self, eyeballing her older sister who pivots her sentence.

"Well, they learned to fear it as evil, if you can imagine that. Natural things from creator Yahu, from the universe, as evil. Mph. So, the law guardians grew stronger, chasing off and even killing people like us. Those who survived faded into culturally acceptable roles as priests, shepherds, wives, and such, forsaking their honed abilities. Ifrah and I settled here."

"And why not?" Ifrah poses as she picks a few tiny, glossy, green leaves off a small khat shrub on the side of the table and clumps them into a little ball, and places it in her mouth, chewing sporadically. "Everything we need to live with vitality, be most creative, and even see glimpses of other realms are in these woods and in these magnificent gifts from the ground. Where else would we want to live?"

I look around the tree house and nod my head. *Where else?* We talk more and laugh often as we eat until our bellies are full. Gullah thanks the universe for the food, clears the table, and shoos us off to bed. I'm ready and quickly drift off to sleep.

The sun is well up when I awake. I feel rested and happy to sleep longer than usual. Moh is in the eating area, mixing salad greens, herbs, spices, and oil. Emah and Ifrah are sipping some sort of drink out in the garden. Gullah is standing outside the house near the forest in front of a large bowl crafted of hammered metal and decorated with a giant, winged beetle. She stirs into it what she later tells me is the blood of a white dove mixed with myrtle, white wine, and ashes of white wood, then pours the mixture into glass jars. She collects them and brings them into the house.

I volunteer to forage wild things for tonight's feast, so I grab a bucket and my sling, returning before the sun starts to fade. Gullah delights in my haul of purslane, chicory, and black mulberries for what she calls her you-will-thank-me tart and sweet mix of greens with olive oil and wine vinegar.

Soon, the sound of the gong rings out. Its echoing pitch calls us together for our new moon feast. Before going out, though, Emah wraps my shoulders with a beige-colored, linen cloak that opens in front and drags the floor.

"Leave your trousers," she says.

"What?"

"Leave your trousers."

"What is this?" She doesn't answer but places a crown of sweet-smelling leaves and vivid flowers on my head and lays my hair over the cape's back hood. *This visit is about me.*

In the garden, four large tree stumps topped with plush cushions are arranged around the carved tree that is now adorned with flowers and greenery and purple ribbons. Along the reed-band table are lit candles, platters of food, jars of drink, and empty goblets. Small lamps and incense-burning pots that radiate the sweet smell of rose petals and myrrh hang along the fence. Ifrah dips a fat wand of dried roses in one of the incense pots and fans its billowing smoke around her body and then around each of us before smudging ash on our foreheads.

Moh, Ifrah, and Gullah, also in hooded cloaks, take their place behind a tree-stump seat. My newly cloaked mother positions me behind a fifth seat. It is a wooden box, about the height of the tree stumps, surrounded by fresh flowers. A hole is cut out of its top, releasing a gentle and pleasantly fragrant vapor. Emah raises the back of my cape and instructs me to sit down on the box. The sensation is at first shocking, then tickly, strangely relaxing, and hotly animated, like the fire that rises along my spine whenever I'm in touching distance of Dawit.

"Stretch out and join hands, please," Gullah starts after taking a long, deep breath. "We stand here to honor you, Abyga'el, daughter of Shmuel, daughter of Zellah, our family, our friend, our beloved. You have grown up strong and beautiful and are now becoming a wife. Tonight, we comprise your sacred circle of preparation and power, wheels within a wheel mutually dependent and on one accord."

We drop hands and Gullah places two fingers on her heart and bows her head. We mimic her as she starts to speak again.

"We welcome you, great Yahu, our infinitely intelligent creator, in unity with the totality of your universe and beseech you to make your presence known in, through, and among us this night. Guide us in preparing your creation, Abyga'el, to meet the dawn of matrimony whole, balanced, and resolute. Likewise, compel our leaders, king, and high priest, to reconnect for the betterment and unity of our people. We know that in you, Yahu, Abyga'el has—and we all have—power, being, peace, and a good future. Let it be so."

"Let it be so," we answer as Ifrah begins to thump her timbrel, leaping and dancing around as we all sing.

> Oneness. Power. Knowing. Yahu in me, all one.
> Om, om peace. Om, om peace.
> Being. Movement. Meaning. Yahu in me, all one.
> Om, om peace. Om, om peace.
> Freedom. Future. Forever. Yahu in me, all one.
> Om, om peace. Om, om peace.

"Yas," Ifrah shouts. "Halal Yahu." This Ifrah is surprisingly more energetic and excited than the one I met yesterday. "I feel that great spirit stirring in here." She spins around and around.

"Yes, yes," Gullah agrees between deep breaths. "Let us resume. Aby, the first part of your circle of preparation is of the body, where you sense the experiences to come in your new union." She hands me a small cup. "Take and drink all at once."

I do and immediately taste the liquid's distinctive bitterness. Chicory juice.

"The chicory," she says, "denotes the unpleasantness you will face as conflicts and hard times arise. This," she hands me a slice of lemon, "is sour. It signifies disappointments in unmet expectations, though I'm sure our dear Zellah is an exception and knows none of this, but not all of us can be wife to the high priest, you know."

"This is not about me," Emah counters.

"Of course, dear sister."

Following the first two tastings is a chili pepper that

stands for the fiery passion of the relationship, at least in Gullah's mind, and lastly, a date dipped in honey that represents the union's joy. *Nice but irrelevant to my arrangement with Nabal.*

"The second part of your circle of preparation is of the mind," Moh announces, standing to his feet. "A mind fixed on love is what will keep you in peace. Aby, in just the short time that we have become what I regard and cherish as friends, I already know that you have a strong heart that guides your thoughts and actions. You are willing to know yourself and to think for yourself in hopes of making decisions to do good. I admire that. Your mental fortitude must be genuine and firm to make the most of this, ah, your union, whether bitter or sweet. Thus, I give you this amulet, carved from rare gems, that contains two reminders for you to guard and renew your mind: a lemongrass stem and a bilberry fruit for clear vision, day or night." He ties the charm to my left wrist and hugs my neck, and I hold back my tears.

"Hey," Ifrah shouts. "I get a hug, too, because I put the invocation on that sweet piece of metal."

"Thank you, Dodah Ifrah," I say, hugging her.

Emah stands and faces me, then starts her speech. "Now, Abyga'el, comes the third and final part of your circle of preparation. The spirit. You know that it is the expression of Yahu inside you, as you, with the ability to transcend space and time. If you allow it. If you recognize and commune with it. If you cherish it enough to keep your body a purified home for it. An essential door to that home is your sacred treasure."

"Emah," I cry.

"None of that," she hushes me. "You and I have talked about this many times and everyone here is conscious, including your newest comrade." She nods to Moh, and he nods back. "Your treasure is a holy portal, a canal of life, of creative good, and of balance, and a gateway to your spirit. It means that the energy therein is spiritual first, then physical. It must be authentic before anyone is invited to transfer his own energy, and not everyone should be allowed to do so. By now, your treasure sealing is complete." She nods to Ifrah who motions for me to stand. She places a solid plank over the wooden box and I sit back down, this time on my cloak, as Emah continues.

"Now, it's up to you to keep it so and prime it for when your husband enters for union and eng—

"About that," I interrupt.

"Yes?"

"I see my arrangement with Nabal as less of a marriage and more of a business deal that provides for child rights. He is just the sponsor of my mission, not my husband nor will I be his wife so consummation must never take place."

"Arrangement?" Ifrah steps closer to me. The others seem frozen. "What arrangement? This is a betrothal, meaning that you're already a wife which means consummation."

"Not the way I see it."

"Then, your seeing is severely flawed," Moh says grimly. "I'm sure that Nabal sees it the way Ifrah just described, and he will not be denied."

"I would think so," Emah agrees. "What would he get out of your, ah, arrangement? Why would he need it?"

"Well . . . he . . . ah . . ."

"Let me tell you what he gets," Ifrah continues. "He gets you for bragging rights and gets your body for physical pleasure."

"Indeed," Moh nods. "That right is of an urgency to

him. It matters not that he is already husband to three wives and a steady suitor of many concubines."

"That cannot happen." My breathing deepens and my body heats up. "I cannot. I do not want to be that way with him."

"Did you not consider that when you agreed to the betrothal?" Gullah asks with force.

Sometimes, a person doesn't think fully about the aftermath of any action until she or he is amongst it, as I am. The betrothal brands me a married woman, legally and in the eyes of my people. I believe what matters to Yahu is my heart, and not consummating the marriage will keep my mind and body pure for another. That is my hope. That is my intent.

"No, not really," I finally respond to Gullah. "Saving the children is my focus and, even then, my heart now desires another so I cannot, I will not, give myself to Nabal."

"Dawit," Emah hums, stepping closer to me and piercing me with her voice. "I knew it was happening. I saw how the two of you looked at each other and floated around each other when he was in Ramah. I warned you about it, didn't I? You are betrothed, Aby, and can have eyes for no one else."

"I can't explain it, Emah, and I can't stop it. I don't want to stop it. I only know it is to him alone that I will give myself. I just need you all to help me figure out how to evade Nabal."

"Your ask is unthinkable," Emah barks. "You want to obtain the land by marriage and remain a virgin? I'm sure it's too late for that. By your own consent and mark, Nabal is your husband according to the law, and consummation—the shedding of blood—is essential before marriage and its betrothal price are official."

According to the law. Those are the same words a perverse Ebre father speaks after beating his daughter senseless simply because she walks from the market alone with the neighbor's young son.

"The law is not all we know, Emah," I say. "We also know the voice and truth of Yahu. The truth is my heart belongs to Dawit."

"That may be, but the agreement you made is under the law, which requires proof of consummation by the morning after your wedding night."

"That is so, my dear Zellah," Ifrah says as she puts a finger to her chin. "But the law does not specify whose blood is to be shed, right?"

"The presumption is that it comes from the virgin who is, at that time, no longer a virgin."

"Yeah, and that could come from Aby or from someone or something else, right?

"What are you suggesting?"

"It's best if I don't say." Ifrah winks her eye at me. "I have a few notions in mind and will come up with a suitable plan for the hungry groom."

"Count me in." Moh raises his hand as if his deep voice isn't enough. "I have earned the trust and ear of Nabal and can easily influence his, well, appetite.

"Excellent," Ifrah claps.

"Since you are orchestrating this performance, Ifrah," Emah says. "I beseech you to escort your niece to Ma'on and be her council there, along with Moh, of course."

"It is done, dear Zellah. I am more than willing and able. Between our garden allies and Moh's influence, we will be sure to keep our Aby whole."

"It seems you have it figured out," Gullah says, then pronounces the end of the discussion and ceremony with a prayer before we eat and dance into the night.

CHAPTER 9

BESET

[be'set]: to trouble or threaten persistently.

TWO DAYS BACK IN RAMAH AND our time in the forest is already a distant memory.

Emah is grumpy or silent but refuses to say why. Tiye detains me in the food house as often as she can, determined to give me tips on meal preparations, as if I'll be doing any of that. Ifrah and Moh are together constantly, like conjoined butterflies plotting how I may best keep my sacred treasure, well, sacred. I spend most of my time preparing Uzi to be back in Ma'on tomorrow. My last day as a resident here is a sadness that I take into my dreams tonight.

Moh is waiting the next morning at the wagon drawn by the two big horses, already loaded with packed clothes, food, and herbs. The wagon's driver is by his side and Uzi is nestled in a make-do stall in the back. "This is it?" He sounds commanding even when he's trying to be nice.

"This is it," I nod.

"This is it," Emah agrees as others look on. "Aby, your father and I will arrive shortly. Remember your time in the circle and that Ifrah is nearby. Think twice and speak once, always truth with love. That is who you are."

"Yes, Emah." I hug her, Tiye, and others, hop onto the wagon, and take a last look at my home as we exit the front gate.

The horses move faster than mules, so the tip of the Ramah gate fades quickly from view. My neck is sore from looking back, wondering when or if I'd ever see it again and how different life will be in Ma'on, in the Desert of Pharan.

Pharan was once home to our forefather, Ishmael, and one of the places where our Eber ancestors sojourned after leaving Misra'yim, the place of their enslavement. I think, again, of the one time I was near there with Abbah.

"Aby," Moh breaks the long silence. "Why can't the children in distress live in Ramah?"

"Hah!" Ifrah shouts. "Not with Shmuel there."

"Why do you say that?" Moh asks with some frustration.

"As the high priest of our people," I start to answer, "Abbah is the primary guardian of our law. People expect him, if no one else, to uphold it and its accepted interpretations that favor adults, even if he is working to change them. If Ramah would become a sanctuary place for abandoned children, then Abbah would likely be found guilty of breaking the law—a status that would beset him."

"That makes no sense. It's not the children's fault. They aren't breaking the law."

"They are in the abuser's mind, especially if you want someone to obey you without question. You know how that works from what you told me about your homeland, right?"

"Yeah," Moh says reluctantly. "It is what it is."

"And it isn't what it isn't," Ifrah adds.

We remain quiet until I ask Moh, "Is Massa really a fool as his name suggests?"

"That is my verdict on his nature, but you are to judge for yourself."

"I doubt that it will matter to me one way or another."

"Easy for you to say that now, but you'll see."

Moh's face droops but I shake it off and crawl into the stall with Uzi. We look out the tailgate, admiring the green scenery, enjoying some food, and appreciating the shade of cover from the wagon.

"Do you like it in Ma'on?" Ifrah starts a chat with Moh.

"I do, as much as I can. Handling Massa and his affairs can be quite demanding. Still, I get to enjoy Massa's toys, like this wagon, the grand horses, the bath services, and other things like that."

"Mmm, bathing services. I like the thought of that."

"I get them whenever I can," Moh answers with a laugh. "Ma'on is in the Y'hudah hills where I like to go and gaze at the wide, rich green pasture lands, the roaming flocks that feed there, and the barren yet artful desert of Negeb. There is much flowing and flowering beauty."

"Like the yellow ribbon hanging off that big rock over there?"

"Stop," I shout and sit up straight.

"What?" Ifrah asks.

"It could mean something."

We assess the boulder and the thick greenery and red poppy flowers surrounding it to discover a girl slouched in tall grass under a nearby skinny cypress tree. She looks to be about eight years old. The braids on her head jet up left and right, like wildflowers blown in the wind. Mucus is caked on her upper lip. Bruises cover her limp arms and legs, likely reasons why she does not wake up when we pat her hand or speak into her ear.

"Is she dead?" Moh whispers.

"No," Ifrah answers. "She is breathing but without any response."

Moh picks up the girl and puts her in the back of the wagon. *Another fallen star.* I stare at the scene—Ifrah caressing the girl's head in her lap and fingering water on her lips as Uzi sits guard—before going up front with Moh and the driver.

"The girl will be Ifrah's daughter until we can determine the best place for her," Moh announces after we start moving again. "She grew tired from the journey and is sleeping. A longer tunic will hide her injuries."

"Another cover-up?"

"For now."

"And her name?"

"Call her Nimtsa," Ifrah calls out. "She was lost but is now found."

We ride on, passing by cave tombs and dirt graves and burning trash pits, until Moh signals for the driver to stop.

"Welcome to Kalebtu, home of Adon Nabal of the Bet Kaleb, of the tribe of Y'hudah."

"We're here?" I want confirmation.

"Almost." Still some distance away is an ornate front gate. Moh hands me a wrapped package. "Here, put this on."

"Huh?"

"It's your betrothal garment as it's clear that you've chosen to ignore the little instruction to be in seclusion and veil yourself in public once you agree to marry."

"Oh, that."

"Yes, that. Even here, it is of concern so don it from head to toe over what you're wearing."

"Of course," I snarl. *The law.*

The thin, airy, white clothing covers my face and feet like a big, billowing tent. Still, I can see that we are pulling up to Kalebtu's main gate. A watchman checks the wagon before letting us pass onto a narrow path and through a second gate that stands opposite a large, round, white building. Its half-sphere domed roof, glistening amid a setting sun, sits atop tall walls and a wraparound porch with thick columns. A layer of white pebbles forms a pathway from the road to the outer and inner courts.

"Look," I say to Ifrah, pointing to the wavy top. "It reminds me of white moonstone."

"Yes," she answers. "But it's golden and like metal instead of stone. It's not gold, is it?" We both turn to Moh.

"It is," he says dryly. "You'll see a lot of it in that building. It is Massa's quarters." *Interesting.* "He calls it 'the palace.' Festivities, when they occur here, happen on the palace lawn. It's where the ceremony will take place."

"What are those?" I point again, this time to sculptures of black birds, one at the top of each thick column.

"Ravens," Moh answers. "They mean something magical, perhaps sinister, to Massa."

"They can be," Ifrah is quick to add, stretching to see them. "More often, they spread good tidings and deliver omens."

"Whatever it is, he believes in it and kisses a large statue of one every morning and night."

The driver steers us onto a road to the right. Ahead are three one-story houses made of mudbrick across the road from the palace. They are homes to Nabal's head cook, head clothes maker, and some of the unmarried female servants. Next to them is a narrow empty plot of land and next to it is a row of five two-story stoned homes. They look the same, except one is larger and slightly more decorated than the others.

We stop at the first look-alike house. Its granite-stoned walkway leads to the front door where a stocky woman dressed in a breezy orange and green tunic and matching headscarf stands with her arms hanging by her sides like an attentive and loyal soldier.

Moh instructs the driver to unload Uzi and our bags, situating them in or around the house, and then take Nimtsa and Ifrah to the town healer. He turns to me.

"This is your new home."

Whatever. I will not cry. I remember why I'm here and redirect my thoughts. Moh and I start our walk to the front door when another woman pops out of the house and runs down the path toward us.

"Moh! You're home. I missed you so much." She hugs and shakes Moh for an uncomfortable while, then embraces me. "And you must be Revi'i, our new and fourth co-wife."

"My name is Abyga'el, not Revi'i. You can call me Aby."

"Of course, may it be as you say," she beams. "I am Pai, daughter of Herut and Salana, but everyone calls me Sheni because I am wife number two. I am here to assist you in your entry to Kalebtu. So, welcome!"

Sheni pulls me into the house, her tall, slim frame obviously stronger than it looks. Moh and the attentive soldier follow us into a large room where a table of bright purple linen and golden platters full of food await. Pickled and dried fish. Smoked and burnt meats glistening with olive oil. Sweet cakes, fried dough, honey nuts, and mellow wines. A scattering of fresh fruits and roasted vegetables. We enjoy it straight away. Well, some of it. I ask Sheni to send a basket of food to the healer's house for Ifrah and Nimtsa, which she directs the soldier to do.

"This is Bentah," Sheni introduces the stocky, now more cheerful woman. "She is your live-in help and can assist you in most anything you need."

"Did you make all this food?" I ask Bentah, who shakes her head as she leaves.

"No," Sheni answers. "We get our food and drinks from a central kitchen on the other side of the palace."

"It is delicious," I say loudly in hopes that Bentah will hear.

"Where is Shlishi?" Moh asks, looking around.

"Shlishi, ah, wife number three . . ." she looks at me, "left nearly a moon ago, shortly after Moh left to receive you, Aby. Her brother is gravely ill, so she went to visit him and take care of some family business." She nods and smiles around at us diners much like the way Abbah does when he delivers a sermon on repentance or Yahu's power or some other spiritual topic.

"I pray everything ends well and that she returns soon." Moh stands abruptly and heads for the door. "Ladies, it is time for me to be gone too. I need to check in with Massa and resume my usual fun duties. Until tomorrow then."

I am left with Sheni and time to relax.

"Where is the healer's house? I want to check on the, ah, daughter of my . . . my handmaid."

"You cannot go out until the time of the wedding. You are the bride and must stay hidden. Surely, you know this?"

"Yes. I forget about that. Forgive me." I pause. "What if I hide under your garment?"

"We both can't fit in mine, Revi'i—ah, Aby."

"No. Of course, not. I mean, let me wear your clothes for a moment so that I can see about my loved ones. I won't be gone long. Please?"

She ponders the idea and eventually agrees, veiling me with her linen cloak in beautifully patterned shades of green, blue, and yellow and showing me the way to the healer's house behind the palace.

"Now, they will think that you are me," she says. "Keep your head down and if anyone speaks to you, answer with, 'May it be as you say.' That's what I say all the time. Come back quickly and tell Bentah when you do. She will know what to do next."

When I get to the healer's house, Nimtsa is still comatose. Ifrah is asleep too. The healer is tending to them both.

"The girl has a significant bruise on her head, it seems, from falling off the wagon according to her mother," the healer says without looking at me. The big sleeves of her many-colored tunic flap around as she warms little bronze glasses and places them mouth-down along the girl's arms and legs.

"Ah, yes, ma'am. Will she be all right?"

"In a day or so. This will better move blood throughout her body and hasten healing. They both will stay with me tonight and you would do best to go back into hiding until your appointed time."

I nod and go outside. The back of the palace is as grand as the front with an equal number of bold columns and such. What doesn't fit is a thick, square stone post some seven feet high that narrows slightly at the top, erected in the side yard opposite one of the ornate porch pillars. Short iron shackles hang on all four sides. I tremble, thinking about the practice that likely takes place there.

The structure to my left looks like it could be a

bathhouse that Moh mentioned earlier. The air around it is perfumed with balsam and other sweet-smelling fragrances. Steam escapes from its open roof. Below the bathhouse, colorful textiles hang over rooftop walls, drying in the sun. Women up there are busy, dying different fibers, spinning them into yarn, and making artful garments and other goods.

I decide to go right and farther around what I now know to be a long, horseshoe-shaped road that encircles the palace. Here and there are open-air, mini courtyards, shaded by tan and brown canvases. At the first one I pass by, four plump women roam around a long, narrow table, stone fire pits, and round clay ovens, grinding grain into flour, baking bread, and roasting meat. Pots, pans, and long-handled tools hang off a wooden frame. It's the central kitchen. Ahead, women empty baskets full of grapes to the floor of a nearby limestone basin where men wait under a covered awning to stomp the fruit into wine. A cluster of olive trees, an ample vineyard, and a sizable garden are backdrops for the dozens of workers, a few of whom pause a second or two to regard me before returning to their tasks. Huts and makeshift homes create a border behind the work activities that occur closer to the road and the palace. Sheep and goats are confined in an enclosed, grassy field behind the gardens; they are many, but not nearly the thousands Massa is said to have.

"Peace, Gebirah Sheni," a guard calls out as I pass by the main gate. "I said peace to you, Gebirah Sheni."

"Oh, may it be as you say," I reply and quicken my pace to hurry back to the safety of a covered roof and Uzi.

"*Tweeeeet-tweeeeet-kola-kola-tweet-tweet-kola-tweeeeet,*" I sing.

Uzi is standing in a large stall in the back of the house,

looking out of a window. His water and food mangers are full, and there is plenty of straw on the floor. His eyes are wide and tense. I start to brush his coat.

"I know it might be scary for you, being back or near this place of your horror, but it will be different because we are together. I've got your back and you've got mine. And I have a surprise for you. Tomorrow."

Just after sundown, Bentah fetches me from my resting place.

"Peace," I offer.

"Peace is only taken. It cannot be given," she counters.

Okay.

She takes me up to the flat rooftop. Oil lamps and pots simmering with frankincense rest on shelves affixed to tall lattices around the roof's edge. Several high awnings allow moonlight yet guard against prying eyes. Large cream and gold drying towels hang from hooks also on the lattices. A couple of narrow benches, covered in white cloths, line the left wall. Steam rises from myrrh-infused water that fills a long stone tub sitting atop a thick, yellow mat on the wooden floor. Bunches of white henna flowers float in the bath water.

Bentah moves quietly and cautiously closer and begins to undress me. She points to the tub, and I submerge. She heats rainwater from the roof's collection jug in a pot over a small fire to keep the ritual bath warm and uses a large spoon to stir the water and flowers.

"You don't say much, do you?" I ask her, softly.

"It is better to listen than to speak."

"This feels like the preparation of a lamb before its slaughter for the spring feast. Is that what this is?"

"It is what you say it is." She spreads her arms toward the massage, combing, hair oiling, and perfuming stations. "As a truth, all this is intended to fluff you up for him, who will partake. And if you so choose, it is also a time for you to purify and ready your spirit for what is about to happen."

"Consummation? Is that what's about to happen?"

"It's bigger than that, and time will tell. Until then, renew your mind, find your heart, and let nothing easily beset you."

She pours water over my head, concluding our chat.

CHAPTER 10

BEVY

[bey-vē]: a large group of people or things of a particular kind

I WAKE THE NEXT MORNING TO Ifrah's fingers tickling the back of my neck. It must be about the third hour, given the angle of the welcomed sunbeams lighting the floor.

"Time to wake up, sleepy girl, you're burning up half the morning. It's your wedding day!" Her giggly greeting doesn't bother me one bit. I feel rejuvenated and rested, despite the strange surroundings. "Come on, girl. Get up, pray, and let's get going."

"Where is everyone else . . . Sheni and Bentah? Oh, and Nimtsa. I must meet her."

"I haven't seen Sheni today and Bentah laid out first meal early. She and Nimtsa await us upstairs."

"Aby, this is Nimtsa," Ifrah says as soon as we step onto the roof. "Nimtsa, this is Aby."

"Not Nimtsa," the little girl says quietly yet defiantly, staring at Ifrah and taking a big bite of her raisin cake. Her cheeks are the color of spicy-orange and her big eyes are bright, detracting from the noise of her visible ribs and sharp collarbones.

"What is your name, then?"

"I won't tell you."

"Well, hello, I won't tell you. I'm happy to meet you."

"Not that either."

"Okay. No worries." I stoop down to hug her, being careful with her frailty. "For now, we will call you 'Nimtsa' because we are happy that you have been found and are rightly situated. Are you feeling better?"

"Un-huh."

"Good. Let's eat."

I pick up a raisin cake. The food is as scrumptious as yesterday's, or maybe I'm just that hungry again. Once Bentah takes Nimtsa downstairs for her grooming, Ifrah comes close and begins to draw designs along my fingers with twigs dipped in purple dye made from mollusks, which fades over time. We laugh and lament as she tells me of her herbal plan to protect my heart and womanhood. She teaches me about the female side of Yahu, of ways to influence foolish men, and of hand and finger movements that hypnotize watchers. The air around us is filling up with conflicting scents of smoldering frankincense and charring meat, exaggerated by the rising heat. Hammering of wood and iron offers a cadence to our chat.

"I'll say this," Ifrah concludes. "As a woman, you have abilities that men do not. Learn to use them as I've taught you. Trust them. The most self-confining decisions I ever made were based on what someone else wanted or thought of me. It's a mistake. Understand?"

"Understood." And as if on cue, Bentah is back to get

me from the roof. The sixth hour is quickly upon us, and I am next on her grooming schedule.

After much pulling, pushing, dabbing, and tapping, Bentah is done embellishing me for the ceremony. I stare but do not recognize the girl in the mirror. Protruding cheeks that shimmer as if sprinkled with gold dust. Full lips plumped more by the potent pigment of red ochre clay mixed with sheep fat. Nose, eyes, and forehead hidden behind a veil of gold leaves and charms dangling from a gold headband with a connected nose chain. Another chain of gold leaves and amethyst stones encircle my neck. Long gold earrings peek out from a sheer, white, fine linen veil that flows from the top of my head to below my elbows where the sleeves of my white tunic, richly embroidered with gold thread, end. A second veil attaches to my shoulders and widens to my sandaled feet, pooling on the floor behind me. A white and gold sash cinches my waist and the amulet from Moh adorns my wrist. A fatted sacrificial lamb of my own doing. Though the outer me is altered, the inner me is the same. I am unafraid.

"The soul does not go the way of the body," Bentah murmurs and walks away. *Whatever that means.*

"That's different," a familiar voice comes from behind me.

"Abbah!" He hugs me gently. "I'm so glad you're here." He is festive in his regal robe and turban of blues, gold, and cream with tassels and ropes, worn on our least holy festival days. I hold onto him tightly, taking comfort in his cottony beard with its spicey-sweet hint of cinnamon and almond oil which he favors.

"Emah," I inhale with a smile, letting go of Abbah. "I've missed you terribly and how gorgeous you are."

"Not me," Emah caresses my chin. "You, dear daughter."

She shines in a tan garb interwoven with red threads of different designs. A matching headwrap tops her head. The last time I saw her dressed like this was at Dawit's wedding to Michal. Now, it's for me.

"Family," Ifrah walks in followed by Nimtsa who is also arrayed in fine beige embroidered linen. "I think it is time to start the procession." She puts a small pouch into the inner fold of my sash and winks before ushering us into the front room where a bevy of more beautiful women in equally beautiful clothing are gathered.

One woman with smooth, coffee-toned skin, high cheeks on an egg-shaped face, long and outstretched neck, and slender arms is standing in the center of the room, chatting with the congregation of handmaidens and female servants. Her attire, including a headdress that cannot contain her long hair, is just as magnificent as mine but in deep, dark colors of purple that make her look tall and slim. Hers also features a broad sash tied around her waist with citrine and sapphire gems that sparkle when hit by sunlight, bedazzling the room in yellows, golds, and blues. A shiny purple pouch swings from a wide, hammered silver cuff on her wrist. Sheni is dressed similarly in vibrant greens but without a pouch. We, it seems, are the co-wives; the third of whom is still absent. As I enter the room, the crowd parts to create a corridor between me and the woman in purple. She prances toward me, her almond-shaped eyes looking left and right with pretentiousness.

"I am Zahra Salome, daughter of Cilmi from the land of Punt." She looks away to smile at our attentive audience and then back to me. "You may call me Rishon, as others here do, because I am the first and chief wife of Nabal, leader of the Kaleb clan, the largest in Y'hudah." The dull voice coming from such a lofty first-wifedom height reminds me of a dark-blue thrush sparrow perched alone on a housetop, moaning. She seems to enjoy that spot, gazing down at me, if only slightly. I get a bit antsy, but maybe this is how she copes with what may be a difficult marital position.

"I welcome you to this, our house," she continues. "Here, Nabal is absolute lord, lawmaker, and judge. Follow him and you will thrive because, here, Nabal is above the king and any other."

"Is he above Yahu, also?"

Ifrah elbows my side.

"You will soon see, Revi'i, and know for yourself."

"I can hardly wait." I move past her and toward the door but stop just before my exit. "And just to clarify, I am Abyga'el, daughter of Shmuel and Zellah from Ramah, but you may call me Aby if you expect me to answer."

Moh is at the end of the walkway, and I hug him tightly.

"Woah." He pushes me back. "Breathe, if you can. Is this the rugged, hill-crawling, slinger Abyga'el whom I met a moon ago?"

"Forever and always."

"You look-look . . ."

"I know. Like a pompous harlot."

"No, no, no. You look like the dignified royalty that you are." He squeezes my hand and points to his left. "And I did as you commanded, my queen."

There is Uzi on the road, standing gloriously with a long white and gold mat covering his back and gold ribbons hanging from his neck, livened by a warm, dry breeze. He appears as uncomfortable as I am.

"Apologies, my friend, but we're in this together," I

whisper and giggle in his ear as Moh helps me mount him. "We will show them who is lord around here."

"Aby?" Emah asks, as the others maneuver in the front yard.

"Get down from that beast," Rishon screams. "You are to stroll with the rest of us. Are you mad? I'm not walking behind that animal."

"Mad like Moshe parting the Yam Suph," I reply and nudge Uzi to start walking. "If you pick up your pace, then I am pleased for you to walk in front." They all do, creating a tinkling concert with their bejeweled anklets.

The procession goes up the road the way of the weavers, the bathers, and the healer. Oil lamps high on building edges send sweet and citrusy scents into the air and illuminate our walk as twilight draws near. Residents wave fig branches and lay palm leaves on the path ahead of us. They throw flower petals in the air and cheer and clap loudly, incited by Rishon's elite nods and finger-pointing. The companion to their merriment is the odd show of annoyance or apathy on their faces.

Once we pass the orchards on our right, the front palace lawn on our left comes into view. Several white and tan tents are positioned on the grounds, offering shade to well-wishers who cheer and clap voluntarily or under compulsion. An elaborate white canopy painted with gold ravens dominates the lawn and musicians begin to play.

A broad, short man dressed in gold and white waits at the end of the pebbled walkway with many companions standing around him, whooping and hollering. *Nabal, otherwise called Massa, no doubt.*

"Behold," he yells and stretches out his arms toward the procession. "A stunning lass on a splendid ass." He claps his hands and turns to the eager congregation who imitate his performance with claps, cheers, and laughs. Attendants stop Uzi at the walkway's end and help me to the ground. The man extends to me his right hand, which sports a large, raven-stamped signet ring on its third finger. A matching garland of small gold ravens encircles his head and golden raven charms swing at the end of his tunic tassels. A thick gold and amethyst necklace hangs on his chest.

"My beloved," the man starts, taking hold of my hand. "I am he. Nabal, your husband and lord of the house of Kaleb. Today, we drink the wedding cup together and initiate our grand wedding supper." He waves and grins to the crowd as we walk up the pathway and into the inner court. "I can't wait to bump you around," he hisses to me.

Bump me around?

We face the local priest who reads the betrothal contract while holding up a wine-filled golden cup stamped with a raven impression. I take a sip when he passes it to me and confirm my agreement with the contract. Nabal does likewise, then places on the middle finger of my left hand a gold ring chained to a gold bracelet which he clasps on my left wrist.

Abbah, Emah, Moh, Rishon, Sheni, and Nabal's head of security stand near us and take sips from a flask of wine, effectively becoming witnesses to our agreement. The priest then pours wine on the ground to the north, south, east, and west as drink offerings to honor ancestors, calling out a few names of those from this area who recently passed away—except for Nabal's mother and father which, to him, would equate to blasphemy.

"Enough of that," Nabal says to the priest.

"Yes, my lord. I'll finish with these la—"

"This is my day." Nabal's already broad nostrils flare

wider, and his hand raises as if to strike the docile man. Gasps echo across our company of guests and Abbah takes a step forward.

"My lord," I say softly and lightly touch Nabal's arm, causing my veil to caress his chin. "Will the elaborate hand of my lord do harm before these people and keep you from being the grand star of this spectacular night, displaying your power to take on another wife? No, you are much too brilliant for that."

"Beauty and brains," Nabal relaxes then beams at me and others, showing off bright teeth underneath two big, mischievous eyes and pointy eyebrows. "I see why you're the prime pick of the Eber women fruit and I ache to taste all of you. Of course, of course," he regroups. "Let us continue, please, sir."

"Certainly so, my lord," the priest replies. "You always know best."

The priest starts again, spurting a few more words before pronouncing a benediction upon us with exhaling relief. Massa extends his signet ring to my lips for me to kiss the raven. I don't, faking an episode of coughing. Once again, people cheer, clap, and toss flowers, and Massa turns around to bow to them. All I can think of is how much I miss the breath and scent of Dawit. Tears run down my face.

"Now, you all start to feast," Nabal hoots at his guests with a hearty laugh as music starts to blast. "And I will do the same, privately." He picks me up and walks through the canopy to the enclosed tent on the palace front porch— Massa's makeshift wedding chamber. "I shall return shortly," he yells to the partiers and speaks less so to me. "Come now! Let me enter you."

The tent is square and full of plump bed pillows. Nabal

is quick to approach me and begin to undo my clothes, but I remember Ifrah's instructions and start putting them in play.

I push him away from me softly and begin to sway left and right to the beat in my head, swirling playfully around him to remove his tunic and constrain him jokingly with my veil. I get far enough from him to remove the pouch from my sash and empty half of the tiny tin vial of pale-yellow plant oil into a drinking goblet. I wet a linen band with the remaining liquid and snake it around Massa's neck, careful not to get any on my skin. Ifrah says that together they should be more than enough to put him into a deep sleep.

I guide him to the largest collection of pillows just as he collapses to his knees and onto his stomach, and undress him from the waist down and cover him with a thin cotton cloth, making the blubbering, bumping, slapping, straining, squeaking noises that sheep and goats make when they mate. I shed my tunic and rip my undergarment for effect and then empty another teeny bottle— this one filled with blood Ifrah pricked from my finger this morning—onto the bed linen. I position my treasure atop the cloth as I lay down beside Nabal.

Massa starts stirring about fifteen minutes later, just as Ifrah said. He yawns and stretches, then flashes a much brighter smile when he sees the disheveled and stained me.

"I guess I did my job, huh?"

When we emerge from the tent, the crowd barely notices. Nabal signals the blowers to sound the trumpet, getting everyone's attention.

"It. Is. Done," Nabal shouts, holding up the bloodied cloth and raising a fist. Claps and cheers erupt again all around the palace. He hands the cloth to the priest who pronounces proof of virginity and an acceptable consummation, and then passes the material to Emah who folds and bags it for safekeeping should any queries later arise.

Nabal struts to Abbah, shooing me off to Emah and Ifrah who stand nearby.

"The deed is done," Nabal says quietly but loud enough for us to hear. "I alone am now responsible for the girl and, as you know, I am well able to provide for her."

"Your marital state has no hold on my fatherhood," Abbah replies. "Abyga'el forever will be my daughter."

"That may be, but she is my wife and to ensure her, ah, wellbeing, I have a request of you."

"Which is what?"

"Forgiveness among our Eber brethren is our custom, as you know. The time limit for such tends to be seven years. For the land. For bondsmen. Even for strange slaves."

"I am not in need of a study on our law, so please get to your point, sir."

"That time has come for Melek Shaul. Pardon his misstep and restore his position with Yahu so that our little princess will remain happy and whole."

"Your madness is as dangerous as our king's is if you think that threats of man mean anything to me. Only Yahu kills and then makes alive. Only Yahu brings low and then lifts. Only Yahu makes poor and then rich again. Should one hair on my daughter's head be harmed, I will return here with the fury of Yahu in my hand. Do you understand my words?"

"I do, and you be sure not to miss mine."

Abbah stares at Nabal before turning away. He shakes hands with Moh, hugs me, Ifrah, and Nimtsa, and departs with Emah for Ramah. It is a bevy of sweet blessings, bitter goodbyes, and a shocking message for me to watch my back.

The wedding revelry of song, music, dance, drink, and smoldering herbs resumes with zest, lasting for seven nights and eight days. Nabal is at the center of the amusement which makes it easier for me to keep up the farce of my marital responsibility.

On day nine, Massa restarts his weekly wife rotation with Rishon and a very fine mix of concubines who are more than happy to share his bed. It grants me a good twenty or thirty days of relief, especially if wife number three returns soon.

CHAPTER 11

BEGINS

[be-GINz]: to come or bring into existence.

I SPEND TIME SEEING MOH IN his executive element, meeting and traveling to manage Nabal and his abundant assets. Ifrah and Nimtsa—quickly becoming the big and little sisters I've longed for—settle in a house between mine and the female servants. In a shared space outback, we create an herb garden that might possibly equal Emah's. Uzi and I explore the community and learn more about its residents, most of whom live in small cabins and tents behind the buildings and farmland, away from the main road.

After about two weeks, Rishon summons me to first meal at her house for what she calls co-wives' training. I am the only other wife in attendance.

She is almost twice my age but looks youthful and vibrant with cold eyes and a crafty smile. Like so many people in Kalebtu of varying hues, languages, ancestry, and birthplaces, Rishon—I prefer to call her by her given name, Zahra—is not Ebre.

Massa's father had traveled by water with his rich and

royal allies from Misra'yim to visit Zahra's rumored-to-be-notable southeastern coastal homeland of Punt where tall and wiry people with elongated heads ran gold mines, farmed incense trees, and captured wild animals, like apes and leopards. Impressed by water travel, gifts of livestock, the promise of lucrative trade, and smooth talk, Zahra's father arranged her betrothal to Massa. She and Massa married four years later, when she was twelve.

As first wife, Zahra directs the co-wives. She also oversees maidservants in their daily domestic tasks, like meals, laundry, and weaving; takes on any other responsibilities that don't belong to Moh, which aren't many; and concocts rituals and brews to ward off evil spirits that she says are preventing her from bearing Massa a son.

"I am first wife. Rishon. Do you understand what that means?"

"That you were the first to marry Mas—ah, I mean, Nabal."

"True. But, beyond that. I am queen, here, and intend to create a legacy of greatness for my, ah, queendom that extends beyond Nabal. People of many nations, calling my name. Calling on me. My face on statues. Do you understand what that means to you?"

"No."

"Then, I will tell you. You can be a part of building my legacy and thrive, getting a few benefits of your own. Simply do as I instruct, and you will—well—survive."

"Survive?"

"Survive. There are repercussions for those who disobey and disrespect Adon Nabal and his queen, but why even take that chance?" She rattles off a list of dos and don'ts for me to memorize and observe. "You are the daughter of the high priest of Eber Y'israel, so I know that you are accustomed to following law and order. Consider this list the law and order of Kalebtu. Sheni, the second wife, can help you adhere to them. Do you have any questions?"

"I do." I sit up straighter and lean into her. "Why do people here call Adon Nabal 'Massa'?"

"That is ridiculous. No one here calls him that and never would. He is called 'lord' only, so remember that and be sure that you do not bring any such beastly misnomer to infest this house or else you will experience your first lesson in how to survive. Anything more?"

"Yes. Survival lesson. Is that what happened to wife number three? I still have not seen her."

"Shlishi is no concern of yours. She is away with her family. Mind your own business and trust my words. The choice is yours."

"Yes," I nod. "It is mine. Thank you for the lovely meal."

"One more thing," Zahra says as I turn to leave. She grabs the back of my hair and slashes it off at the nape,

"Argghhhh," I scream and turn around to see the bulk of her teeth protruding in her wide mouth. I reach back and feel nothing, but my neck and short curls coiled in shock. "What have you done?" I lurch forward to plant my right fist into her face but three of her handmaidens stop me in full swing and hold me back.

"This is in case I have to do a few holy rituals of my own as the first wife and high priestess of Kalebtu," she cackles and walks away.

I run out of her house to mine two doors down. The few people still outside after hearing the noise act as if they do not see me. I stop at Uzi's stall and find comfort in the rise of his belly and the warmth of his straw, too furious to cry.

"I am starting to understand what you experienced here and why you hate this place," I whisper to him. "Because of Zahra, the glory of my coat, my crown, is dull. But yours no longer is and mine will return. For Massa and his first wife, retribution is coming. It is already on the way, and I hope that I am around to witness it."

"*Tweeeeet-tweeeeet-kola-kola-tweet-tweet-kola-tweeeeet*," Uzi says and knocks his nose against my cheek, snorting hot breath in my face. He then strikes the post of the stall with his hoof.

"Yes, my friend." We both rise. "That's it. That's us. Our pact is to be there when help and strength are needed. Let's show that strength now."

With a scarf fixed to my hair, I mount Uzi and we roam the estate, greeting people loudly and joyfully, and trotting past Zahra's house as if nothing happened, determined that her beastliness will not reinvent me. After ten or more tours to date, we haven't yet found any throwaways nearby. That may be good, but we continue to look for them.

My early morning begins with a proposition from Moh: accompany him on a trip to the Yarden, south of Kalebtu. While there, we will explore my large-enough land, the harvest of my marital contract. Ifrah forbids our leaving without her and Nimtsa.

"Imagine the herbs I could transplant here from there," she argues with joy.

We journey first to Karmil, about a half-hour ride northwest of Ma'on, where Massa herds his more than three thousand sheep and conducts his substantial wool trading business.

Moh is to drop off some sort of ovine nutritional feed to the head sheepherder there. His proprietary blend of grains, hay, and herbs greatly increases both the density and fineness of Massa's wool. Where most wool producers get one shekel of silver for twenty pounds of wool, Massa gets one shekel of silver for five pounds of what he calls king-worthy wool.

Ample water stored in huge reservoirs, a friendly terrain, and beautiful broad pastures make Karmil and its surrounding wilderness the best plateau in the Y'hudah region. Arriving day visitors see acres of fenced, lush pastures sprinkled with massive dots of black, white, and beige sheep, most belonging to Massa, and plain tan and brown tents here and there.

I gawk at the scenery as the others ride ahead.

Just inside the gate of Har Mihamon, Massa's "hill of wealth" and second estate in Karmil, is the monument to Melek Shaul. The limestone statue must be three times my height—eighteen feet or so—and has the image of Shaul holding a sword over the head of a slain man. An inscription overtop reads, "Shaul, ha-Melek, triumphs over Amalekite foes." I vaguely remember Abbah and Emah talking about the shameless trophy of disobedience when Shaul first erected it years ago after his perceived battle victory at Amalek. Admirers and reluctant supporters still place flowers and charms around the shrine to pacify the king.

"So, Massa and Shaul are friends?" I ask Moh.

"I'd say so. The king is here often. He likes the natural water springs and the thriving vineyards, not to mention the brazen attention from wealthy landowners." The expanse of flocks and lavish entryway into Har Mihamon are milk-and-honey impressive, almost distracting me from Moh's tour narrative. "Karmil was Shaul's first stop on his celebration visits after what he called his complete defeat of the Amalekites. He built the monument in honor of that win, though some say it wasn't a win at all. Massa hosted a festival of gifts, food, drink, and dance to celebrate it with other bigwigs in Karmil. The bash lasted three days and three nights."

The primary house, made of mud and stone, is not the centerpiece of the community like the one at Kalebtu, though it is just as large. It sits at the top of a gigantic ring of other buildings, like a brilliant diamond on a king's crown, encircling acres of grassy fields that Massa uses to host his lofty festivals, notably sheep shearing in early summer. The earthy house has two fronts — one facing the main gate and one facing the interior court. Both sides feature a wide red door with a black raven painted at its center, anchored by stone columns, and surrounded by a raised cobblestone porch. A young man waits for Moh on the porch of the gate-side front.

"This is Ibo, son of Ofer, from Geba," Moh introduces us, and we greet one another. "He is a valuable shepherd in Nabal's business, supervising some of the men who make sure the sheep are protected, graze the best pastures, drink from good waters, and take their vitamins. His work determines the amount of profit Nabal can gain at shearing time." Moh hands Ibo two large pouches of liquid and reminds him of how best to administer it to the flock. Ibo nods his understanding and goes back into the house.

Moh walks me around the estate before we catch up to Ifrah who is chatting with other workers while Nimtsa picks daisies nearby. Only men live here as Massa believes business is a man's job and dictates that women stay in Kalebtu, except for certain festivals. I especially appreciate the available drinking water, rich soil, and aromatic cedar trees—advantages I hope to see on my land in Yarden. I'm eager to go and find out. We repack Uzi and four other donkeys with water, food, bedding, tents, and a few more goods and head out again, this time going south.

After almost a day of walking and resting and riding down winding slopes—past sparkling sapphire blue water, artful ripples of dusty white waves of salt, wide and curvy salt flats steps, and mini salt sculptures of various shapes—we reach the southeast shore of Yam ha-Melah, the salt sea. Salty. Calm. Lifeless. Pale crystal flakes, blown by a light breeze, tickle my face and burden my eyelashes as I admire the golden sand under my feet.

"This is it," Moh proclaims. He looks down as his finger scrolls across a page of a thin, battered book. "Opposite Yam ha-Melah, east of the center of the south-ernmost tip of the salt-water sea." We simultaneously turn around to face the land behind us. "This is it."

We walk and weave around sand dunes held steady by grayish-green broom bushes, then climb the sandy hillside that extends east from the seashore and rises steadily to the edge of a plain about four hundred feet above the lake of salt.

The bigger-than-I-thought slice of tan heaven in front of us rests sleepily beneath a wide, rocky mountain that stands guard over it. The soil, like most in Y'israel in sum-mertime, is parched from little rain, high heat, and dry winds. The lowland is littered with salt-dusted twigs and branches along a worn fence. Half-buried broken clay pot handles, a corner of a large structure, and other remnants of thriving settlements long gone dot the bare area.

"According to this copy of the certified deed of sale, this place is Qasheh." Moh studies the book again. Massa's father traded with a tribal leader from Edom flock and textiles for the thirty-three acres of land many years ago and had the section surveyed, deed transferred, and asset entered into the family records.

"Where is this?" I ask. "Y'hudah?"

"It doesn't seem so." Moh looks at the book again. "I think it is a lot between the Y'hudah wilderness to the west and Moab or Edom to the east. Maybe land that Edom never annexed. I don't know."

"Still, it is just outside the Eber Y'israelite territory and its laws."

"Yep."

"Why didn't Massa keep it for himself?"

"Look at it." Moh scans to his right and left. "Compared to nearby allotments, it is small and insignificant to him. It is like him, hard, cruel, and obstinate, not to mention the inability to drink that seawater."

"It doesn't mean that something wasn't here and can't be here again. When you're looking with those"—I point to Moh's big brown eyes—"you might see nothing. But when you look with your heart, many things come into view. A sanctuary; a glorious sanctuary. Even here."

I walk farther onto the land, envisioning out loud what will be. A wide, salt-graveled walkway stretching from a barrier some twenty feet from the southern shore's bank to inside the land. A massive stone wall surrounds the large sanctuary community. Acacia trees heavy with yellow flowers stand on both sides of an arched entry gate and watchtowers. Tamarisk trees give shade to people inside the gate who enjoy a spacious, stone-paved courtyard with bench seating and a hewn altar to Yahu. Throughout the estate, white broom and bean caper shrubs and evergreen saltbushes help prevent soil erosion and offer tasty flower buds or young leaves to eat. A sizable cistern for any possible rain collection and a well connected to natural freshwater springs deep down serve as sources of water. A large sleeping house is off to the right of the courtyard and a similar one is off to the left. Between them is a long cooking and eating tent. Behind it blooms a host of saline-tolerant crops, like asparagus, coconuts, pomegranates, dates, figs, palms, and artichokes. Opposite the garden are sheep, goat, and donkey pens. A flourishing oasis set upon a hill.

"Perfect," I say. "And somewhere, maybe over there, we will produce a trade, perhaps mineral salts, to sell to the world."

"And herbs," Ifrah adds and claps. "Don't forget the herbs."

"That's certainly a vision." Moh isn't convinced. "A really, really big vision."

"Maybe—but I can feel it. From now on," I start to declare, "this place will be called Bet Tsur because, like an immovable rock, Yahu has already fortified the sanctuary, my vision, for the children who need it. Today, Bet Tsur begins."

We make a small fire from dry white broom wood, set up a tent that covers our faction, spread blankets on the ground inside it, and settle down to rest.

"How can you achieve all of that?" Moh asks out of the blue.

"I can't," I answer sincerely. "But Yahu, whom I serve, can. Along with you, of course." I laugh and hum myself to sleep.

Early the next morning, we pack up and head west around the sea. Just as we turn north toward Ma'on, movement in the dried bushes of the shoreline dune hooks our attention. Moh raises his right fist, signaling for us to stop and be quiet. As Moh's feet hit the ground, so do mine. Ifrah guards her daughter.

With weapons in hand, we ease our way to the shrubbery from where a faint, but constant whimper is coming. Under the brush is a boy. He looks to be about five, but given his puny arms, swollen ankles, and bloated belly, he might be older. The last finger on his left hand is bent backward and bruised. He shrinks as far back into the salty sand as he can go until Moh extends to him water and pomegranate juice. He reaches out for both jugs and drinks hurriedly, relaxing with each swallow, his feet gradually falling to the sides.

We watch the boy refresh for a few moments longer before inquiring about his name, his family, and his circumstance. He stares at us with his big, round, dark, and slightly sunken eyes, but never utters a word. We tear one of our cotton sleep covers into long strips to brace his finger and swaddle him to Nimtsa on her donkey, and then continue our journey north to Kalebtu.

"Seth," the lad says, startling us as Moh unstraps him upon our arrival home.

"Huh?" Ifrah asks in as puzzling a tone as I feel.

"My name is Tafari Seth. I have no father."

"Well, hello there, Tafari Seth," I say and introduce the others. "Welcome to Kalebtu."

"You can just call me Seth," he says, after drinking more juice.

CHAPTER 12

BEASTLY

[bēs(t)lē]: extremely unpleasant.

I BEGIN WORK ON BET TSUR with help from Lami-Yaj, a large man and Kalebtu resident with bulky arms, smooth ebony skin like Zahra's, and short, bushy black hair that stands up from his face. It turns out that he is an expert in civil engineering.

Lami-Yaj was managing the structure design and overseeing construction for large community developments in Nubia and Misra'yim when his employer put him up as a guarantee against a hefty loan from Massa. When the employer failed to pay, Massa brought Lami-Yaj here to work off the debt. That was three earth revolutions ago and the loan is still outstanding. Now, he runs Massa's wine and oil press systems, making them more proficient and, thus, more profitable.

I force him to take sixty ounces of silver each week—a small part of monies I receive regularly as a wife's legal share of the estate—for his Bet Tsur work, knowing that he gets no pay from his community duties and seeing the critical value he is contributing to the sanctuary. We comb through information in the property deed and survey records to develop the site plan, building blueprints, and material requirements.

Like most other villages in Kanaan, Kalebtu can be dry and dusty in late spring and summer. Rock-hewn cisterns, wells, and other man-made pools provide water for drinking and irrigation. From a shady spot at the top of a limestone hill that rises above and far behind the palace, I can see that the wooden and woven fence surrounding the compound roams far and wide, protecting hundreds of goats that feed in the back pastures, separated from the thousands of sheep and lambs that graze nearby in Karmil.

Nabal was born here, on the land developed by his father. The father he is rumored to have killed for insulting his mental abilities. He now owns it all. The land, the buildings, the crops, and—in his mind—the people. You'd think that would make him one of the happiest and most agreeable people in Y'israel. Yet, in my nearly seven moons here, he continues to prove true one of Abbah's many proverbs: The fool has no capacity for wisdom.

Just yesterday, I listened under the oak trees as he formed an official police unit of fifty men to enforce a curfew of twilight. He is convinced that someone steals his wine at night and is now committed to doing everything he can to catch the thief and tie him to the whipping pole. The restriction is in force until the culprit is caught, which I doubt will ever happen. The only ones guilty of depleting the wine is Massa and his companions.

Massa frequently growls orders and penances, like a mad dog fighting over the last bone, at any sign of imagined disrespect, dissent, or insult. "Stupid!" "Disgusting." "Get them out of here!" "To the pillory!" "Burn 'em!" With each brutal shout and bizarre blame, the anxiety level of the compound surges.

One day, Nabal tied up four male residents to the inside posts of the front gate. He said they had stolen vegetables from the estate's garden. Produce, he says, belongs to him to do with as he pleases but certainly not for bandits. He first stripped the men down to their loincloths and had honey slathered over each man. Then, he sprinkled over them the dug-up mounds of red fire ants. The men cried and yelled for five days. I snuck to them at night with water to clean them or give them drink. It did little to help. They died from sting allergy, dehydration, infection, heat, or some foul combination of the four. It was torture for them and a hard message for the rest of us.

And Massa is harsher when his stomach is full of strong drink like it is tonight.

As a servant girl from the cooking tent is pouring wine at Nabal's meal table, one of his henchmen stretches out his arms, bumping the girl, and causing her to spill wine all over Massa and his prized purple robe.

"Stupid girl!" He jumps up and throws his goblet at her, striking her head. "Look what you've done. You will be punish—"

"*Ahh, ahh, ahh,*" I stand up and start to sing and dance for the first time in Kalebtu to distract Massa and allay his anger. "*Ahh, ahh, ahh.*" A hush falls over the crowd and Massa sits back down. Drum and lyre players join me in the performance.

My body twirls and twists and swings and sways, moving freely as the rhythm rises higher and takes with it my breath, heartbeat, and temperature. The span of my hair blossoms. The top of my outer robe slides down to my elbows, exposing my shoulders to the evening desert air. Sweat rises at my neck and trickles down between my breasts.

Hands clap, voices cheer, eyes pop, and mouths open at the sensing of my joy. Especially Nabal's. His gawk turns into a salivating smirk, and he is unable to keep still, suggesting awareness of his own joy between his legs and that his fury over the wine spill is forgotten.

"Stop that!" Zahra screams at me. "Stop it now." The entire assembly grows silent again as she turns around to face Nabal. "Will you sit here and allow this seductress to flaunt her body and skin to embarrass your name? Embarrass me, your first wife?"

"Sit down, woman. The girl is simply providing me and all of us the pleasure of her dance."

"At what cost, my lord? Your strength? Your reputation? Your respect as a man who can no longer cage his wives?"

"Careful, or you will know my uncaged strength right here, right now."

"Will these watchers know it, or will they know your weakness?" She fails to sweeten her tone. "Are you still lord in Kalebtu or is it this . . . this temptress?" He glares at her and then the spectators as the veins in his forehead swell and pulsate.

"I am lord in this place and will always be, and that means lord over you, you witch, so shut up. Sit your butt down, and let this party continue. Why? Because I am lord." He claps his hands, and the musicians start to play again.

Zahra signals her servants, and they stomp off. I head back to my house to compose my appearance. As soon as I turn left to go back up the road, two men rush forward, grab my arms, and begin to pull me back onto the palace wall.

"Take your filthy hands off me!" I strike the knee of

the man on my right with my heel, and he falls to the ground, letting me go. I swing around to punch the other man's nose with my right palm when his fist meets my head.

CHAPTER 13

BEFRIEND

[be-friend]: to become or act as a friend.

"OWW." I RAISE UP ON MY left elbow and wince at the burning pain running up both my arms. A gust of grainy dust flies across my face and though I struggle to think clearly, I am grateful that the air is somewhat cool and the ground beneath me is soft and dry, like sand. Dry, well sand. I push my aching back and pounding head against the well's wall, hoping deep breaths will lessen the pain. I hold my left hand and feel a thick bandage wrapped around my throbbing pinkie finger. "Whew," I exhale the pain.

"It's just a little hurt, girl," a soft, small voice breaks the dead silence. "Toughen up. It will soon pass."

"Who's there?"

"I am you, about eighteen moons ago." She sounds like I feel. Weak. Broken.

I am you? Odd. "Where are we?"

"You don't know? You didn't see?"

"No. No, I didn't see. The last thing I can remember—*oww*—is a large fist zooming toward me."

"Zahra's goons, I'm guessing?"

"Likely. It must have knocked me unconscious."

"Yeah, you were." A little empathy is coming through her tone. "You know where the bathhouse is, right?"

"Yes."

"The mouth of a cistern is several feet behind the bathhouse, enclosed in a cone-shaped tent and disguised as a dry hot room reserved for Massa's use only. We are in the chamber of that tank."

The voice is near, seeming to bounce off the wall to my right so I reach out, moving the air and preparing to navigate the dark dungeon. "*Ooouuuchhhhh*"

"Oh, I see. You're a weakling."

"I've never been called that." I retreat to the wall for comfort.

"A first for everything."

"How do you know that I am new to—"

"Oh, I remember well the betrothal baths. The warm water. The spicy-sweet sense of myrrh that soothed me into a deep sleep. It was my favorite part. Don't you like them?"

"I guess."

"Of course, you do, girl. It's okay to admit it. That's why you're still doing it. I welcomed the scent of myrrh joyfully when yours began to fill this space. And your hair. Your curls remain smooth, soft, and bouncy. Your bronze skin is still supple like the finest linen, except of course for the scratches and bruises you picked up when they tossed you down here. There are no scars on your narrow nose nor gashes on your lips. They remain tawny and plump, for now."

"You have seen me?"

"Seen and touched. It is my sworn duty as supreme

custodian of the cistern to inspect all things that enter herein." She claps her hands and laughs, appearing free for a moment. "The triangled tent was open and the moon was full when they put you in here about two days ago."

"Two days?" I look up and the pitch blackness of the well's throat is deafening.

"Two days."

"I know it was evening when I went lifeless. *Ouuccchhh*! What happened to my finger?"

"It was bleeding when you came down. Looks like it was chopped off at the top or something. I wrapped a linen strip around it."

I hold and rub on it. "How long have you been here?"

"I am guessing two moons?"

"Two moons?" Shock escapes my lips and my heart sinks. "You are Shlishi, wife number three."

"That's what they call me, but that's not what I own. I am Ahinoam, daughter of Hilkiah, of Yizre'el, may Yahu bless his long-departed soul."

"I am Abyga'el, daughter of Shmuel, of Ramah."

"Ahhh, I knew you were the princess of Y'israel."

"No, that would be the king's daughter."

"Close enough."

"I beg you to come near and befriend me so that we may be companions. That way, you may call me Aby."

After a while, I hear her approach slowly and then feel her breath on my shoulder as she sits near me. I reach out, but she pushes my hand away.

"It's me," she says quietly. "I am here, and I will call you Aby."

"And I will call you Ahi." We giggle slightly and sit quietly in the dark.

"Since you have been dumped here like me, then you

are likely different from the others and you might be willing to help me."

"Help you do what?"

"Kill our husband."

"Count me in," I declare. "But first, any chance you have a lamp or torch down here?"

"For what?"

"To better see and talk with you."

"We're talking already."

"Yeah, but we can talk better when I can see your eyes which I'm sure are a lovely shade of red. I mean, why else would they leave you down here?" She laughs.

"Think you can make it over to my corner of this wonderful world?"

"I can, if you help me."

I hold onto the hem of Ahi's long tunic with one hand and feel the rough wall with the other as I shuffle along the floor, painfully blundering over small pebbles the short distance. She settles me down against another wall and moves away to fiddle with something. Clicking and scratching sounds come from her direction and, in a moment, a spark breaks through the dark and she sits a flame atop a candle stuck in the dirt.

"Welcome to my home," she says.

Stones that line a small slice of the curvy wall appear dimly as do the small patch of dirt floor with a pile of figs and grapes gathered on a piece of cloth and a collection of what looks like tiny wineskins lying nearby. A thin, weak arm moves in front of the light. Cloudy-white patches blot its terrain, from the fingers to past the elbow, like goat's milk swirling around in roasted coffee. I slither back further into the wall.

"Don't be afraid. If you could catch it, you'd already have it, but you can't catch it, so you don't have it."

"What . . . is . . . it?"

"It's my skin," she answers with frustration. "It feels the same. It acts the same. It is just becoming without color. See?"

I reach out and touch her bony arm. "I see."

She moves the candle across her sunken but innocent face where white patches encircle her mouth and one of her big, bold eyes. She then puts the light back on the ground. "And no, I don't know why it is happening. Perhaps, it's Yahu's penalty for my being married to a fool or wanting to kill said fool or speaking ill of my brother, my only remaining family, who sold me into this difficulty for the big fat price of two sheep, a goat, and the sheer satisfaction of irresponsibility so he could go join a trade caravan."

We both stare at the ground for a while to dispel the awkwardness and soon our quiet turns into sleep.

The screech of moving iron wakes us. My eyes squint at sunlight beaming down from up top and bouncing off the floor and walls. Several pieces of fruit and water pouches plop onto the well's sandy bottom.

"Hey!" I yell, hoping to catch someone's attention and garner help to get us out. No reply comes. We gather up our goods and eat. I roam around our rocky prison, searching for hints of escape.

"You know, it's not about what a person looks like," I say.

"The hell it is. Did you grow up under a rock in the dark?"

"Nooo." *I had to think about the answer for a second.* "Consider our king who most agree is a very handsome man. Abbah said folk once thought that an invisible halo shined down upon him. But look at what he's doing now.

Disobeying Yahu's way, tearing our nation apart, and hunting down his most loyal guardian to kill him for no good reason."

"I heard about that. Dawit is his name, right?"

"Right. So, a person's appearance is topical, skin deep, and easily changed, often for the worse. Courage, honesty, equity, compassion, humility—things like that are what counts. They last."

"Well, good luck finding those when money and wealth are involved." We laugh and sigh. "And look at you." Ahi's voice is patient.

"What about me?"

"You wouldn't be here if you didn't look like you do."

"Like what? Like you?"

"Be for real. You look like natural royalty."

"Now, you be serious."

"I am. Before I came to Kalebtu, maybe I would say that we both resembled, well, the rumored great beauty, queen Nefertari of Misra'yim." She fixes her neck and hands in the way of queens. We laugh even more and take sips of water.

"I thought you were freaking dead," she disrupts the long silence. "That they had dropped down a corpse to torture me and cause me to go mad or even kill myself, but they would have been wrong. I would never do that to myself. I've been through abuse, starvation, near death, and essentially being sold, but that still did not happen. I would not allow it or any situations that would bring it on, you know? I could not act toward anything close to that."

"What did you say?"

"I've been through abuse, starva—"

"Before that."

"I . . . would . . . never . . . do . . . that . . . to . . . my—"

Her words penetrate a dark depth of my heart.

"Oh my, oh my, oh my." I sink into the sandy floor, choking on the dust as I sob.

"What?" Ahi screams. "Aby, what is it? What—"

"That's-that's-that's it," I cry out.

"What's it?" Ahi hands me a strip of linen that she saved from the tokens sent down to her.

"I am self-inflicted," I cry.

"You are what?"

"My going against our culture to arrange my own betrothal," I say between blowing my nose and wiping my eyes.

"You did what?"

"I am in this cistern by my own hand."

"I don't understand."

"My becoming betrothed to Massa without my father's consent. My . . . my roaming the hillsides of Kanaan alone to find children in distress. My wanting to be at war against Y'israel's enemies. But all of it . . . every bit of it was not sacrificial. It was self-inflicting recklessness, testing fate."

"Self-inflicting?" She holds my hand, her brows raised and eyes wide. "Testing fate?"

"Me, in some stupid way, punishing myself for being born a girl—the gender that gave my birth mother the reason to abandon me. For Abbah and Emah having to take me in. Like I owed my life for all of it." The tears gush, flooding my cheeks and filling my nose with phlegm.

"You're as crazy as a drunken goat, girl. They did not have to take you in. You don't know why your birth mother did what she did, but whatever the reason, how could it be any fault of yours? You were just a child. And you were found. And you were saved."

"But why?" My tear faucet still flows. "What was so special about me?"

"You were alive. And innocent. And deserving of love, like everyone . . . well, except for our husband and maybe his first wife." Ahi giggles and I welcome her humor as sweet relief.

"I hated myself for not being worthy of my birth mother's love," I confess slowly, quietly. "I hated my mother for not fighting for me. I hated our Eber people and law for cultivating the ugliness of caste and separation."

"Dang. That level of hate was bound to come out as craziness."

"Crazy. Insolence. Defiant. Pick one or two. It was how I blindly demonstrated my right to be here, I guess. By hurting the people who truly loved me."

"You didn't know," Ahi says after moments of silence. "Now, you do."

"I guess."

"So now, let go of the craziness. Plain and simple."

"I guess."

"But before you do, let's kill our husband first. Afterward, you can shed all that nasty angry stuff, okay?" There's her humor again.

"Well, before we can get to that and live free of his dead weight, we must find a way to get free from this cistern."

"I'm with that."

We drink water and sit still awhile before Ahi snuffs out the little flame. I sniff and sigh into another night's sleep, waking this morning with clarity of my truth, calm courage, and a warm smile.

"Moh doesn't know you're here," I say.

"I don't think so. He had left on business and then to get you in Ramah when I made my entrance into this charming cave of a kingdom."

"Zahra and Sheni—or Pai, I'd rather call her 'Pai'— said that you had just left to visit your sick brother."

"Zahra's lies. Pai repeats them because she believes them, bless her heart. She's only trying to—"

"Survive," we say together, imitating Zahra, then chuckle.

"It's likely that no one talks about my being down here, but at least Zahra's two goons and one or two other people know," Ahi continues. "Someone from the kitchen, I think, who occasionally drops the fruit and water pouches every two or three days, like the other day. An oily ointment came one day, maybe from the healer, to calm whatever ailments she assumes I have contracted in here. One morning, I found a long scarf bunched up on the ground at the bottom of the pit."

"Moh is in Karmil right now but should be back soon. We can find a way to reach him, and I know that he will do something about getting us out."

"Maybe. His hands are often tied even if his heart is in the right place. He, too, must survive Massa. You know we call him that, yes?"

"Moh told me," I answer. "Our oppressor and our burden."

She nods. "Zahra too."

I spend the day scooting around and crawling on the ground to more finely inspect my new home while Ahi reorganizes our pantry and sleeping spaces. What I think are only rocks scattered about in the dirt are also various types of broken, cracked, and whitened bones. Animal or human? I don't know, but it tells me that beings other than bugs have died down here. There must be a way to get out.

"What do you know about this cistern?" I ask Ahi while feeling the space for moving air. "Did you hear anything about it before you were put here?"

"No. Nothing. There is no outlet, oh wise one. I'm distressed, not stupid. I've tried."

"We're not that far from the co-wives' houses so maybe there's a way that we can dig into the ducts underneath them?"

"I doubt it, but, hey, maybe your highness can come up with something, but let's try at sunrise when it will be lighter, and we can better see. Besides, it will give you a chance to rest and heal a bit more. Deal?"

"Deal."

We repeat our now familiar evening ritual. Remove our top tunics and roll it up to cushion our necks and heads. Extinguish the candle flame, putting us back in the dark. Welcome morning with hopes of more treats, then commence our day of meals, conversations, and meandering in the cavern.

"Ahi, I can name several reasons why you'd want to, but is killing Nabal really your aim?"

"It is. He is a hyena of a husband." She hesitates. "Maybe. I don't know."

"What would you gain from it? Prison or worse, your own death?"

"I wouldn't do it in an obvious way. It would be, you know . . . an accident. Yeah—he would accidentally fall off his horse and into a deep hole just like this one." She snickers. "Aside from that joy, I would gain freedom. Not like leaving this dungeon, but like living as I please."

"We will start to do that as soon as we get out," I prophesize. "As much as we can."

"There's always that, huh?"

"Yes. I'm all for breaking rules, but now I will do it the way Abbah has been urging me all along: more wisely."

"Subservient and with a man, you mean."

"Not necessarily. Probably. If it works . . ." I pause, imagining Dawit. "Best if it's the right kind of man. A rulebreaker himself who is wise, kind, strong, loving, brave, handsome, and even sensual. One who is happy to protect, provide for, and love a wife and their children, even a girl child."

"Oh, please permit me to visualize that for a moment." She hums and moans briefly. "Now, get up, wet those hands, and let's gather enough dust to make such a god and ask Yahu to blow into him the breath of manliness. Just for us." We roll over laughing and my insides dance at her humor, knowing that such a being already exists and is possibly within our reach. Our talk of dreams ends in serenity and sweet sleep.

CHAPTER 14

BETWIXT

[bĭ-twĭkst']: in an intermediate
position; neither wholly one thing nor another.

EARLY SUNRAYS POKE THROUGH THE METAL trellis-covered cistern cover. The tent is open but not the cover and I relish the constant light. It gives me a better look at my sleeping roommate. Except for her matted hair, dirty clothes, boniness, and un-coloring skin, Ahi looks like me and Pai. Coppery brown. Big eyes. Ocher lips. Stack of hair. Thick in the right body parts; thin in others. Massa's type, I suppose.

I fight a swollen ankle and knee to limp quietly underneath the shaft, hoping to find anything to use as steps to the top. Nothing but dust and faded water lines. Without limestone plaster, the surfaces of the shaft and the small, boxy entry room are dry and cracked. On the twenty-feet-plus walls of the larger chamber, where Ahi sleeps, are drawings of houses, work scenes, people, and people's names. If this ever was a water storage tank, it dried up long ago. I suspect it is now a holding place for naysayers and troublemakers, like us. Once again, I begin my search for an out, touching the wall on my left, feeling as high as I can for hidden openings.

"Not used to the accommodations yet?" Ahi jokes with a yawn and a stretch.

"Good morning to you too."

"Good morning. I mean, this is not quite the place for the daughter of our high priest."

"As you now know, I wasn't always that."

"How did you come to be that?"

"I was four, alone, hungry, and passed out on the edge of the main road in Na'aran, a town in the lower east side of the Efrayim territory and a short ride to Gilgal where Abbah and three of his aides were heading on his national tour. I remember my birth mother slinging a cotton scrip over my shoulder with a little food, tunic, and knife in it. She told me that I was on the way to my next family, hugged me, and put me on the back of a donkey behind the man who shared our house. We rode for about half a day before he slid me off the donkey to the side of the road and told me to walk straight until the road ended. It never did."

"Damn."

"Yep. I don't recall the man ever touching me in a wrong way. Abbah found me on that road and took me with him on his tour and then to live with him and Emah in Ramah. So, no, I'm not the princess of Y'israel. I'm just one of a few Ebre orphans who lived."

"You're more than that. You're a woman willing to do hard things to change this world for the better, one child at a time. So, what are you going to do this day to help this child?" She points to herself.

"Find a way out of here. I know there must be a way out."

"There is none, except through the unreachable shaft which, as I said before, is hidden and private to others. Besides, no one is looking for it. Who in their right mind would want to go to a dry hot room in the middle of a desert?"

To keep prisoners alive.

We decide to eat something and rest up before resuming our search. Ahi works the right wall of the chamber. I finish the left wall and turn right to do the back wall. I near its end, meeting Ahi there with no space betwixt us.

"Nothing," she confirms. "Just as I said."

"It looks like the chamber ends, but it does not. Feel that."

She runs her hand over the seam where the two walls appear to meet. "Air."

"Air."

We hit and pull on the wall corners, expecting chunks of wall to dislodge and set us free. When they do not, we dig under the fake corner wall joint with our hands, taking breaks here and there to rest, eat figs, and drink water. On our fifth or sixth round, the left bottom corner of the back wall detaches from the ground and breaks when I hit it hard with a stone, revealing its secret: a long, twisty passage cluttered with beefy and jutting rocks.

Carrying the lit and pouch-contained candle, we carefully tread the path which we deduce is steering us south of the bathhouse. Its floor level rises slowly as we go. We stop frequently to note any familiar sounds from above. When the ceiling is low enough for us to touch, we try different areas for fragile roofing and soil. One jab drops a bit of dirt and gravel onto Ahi's head and shoulders. She punches again and her hand greets the open air. The hole is about the size of a mature pomegranate and isn't getting any bigger despite our efforts.

"We need help," Ahi says, straining to look through the hole.

"Yeah, the right help. What can you see?" Our location could mean freedom or new confinement.

"Not much. Some greenery and some light. Based on our travel here, we are likely near Pai's house, next door to mine, underneath the row of oak trees."

"Maybe. What hour might it be?" I ask nervously.

"I've been down under so long that it'd be hard for me to say. Ninth, maybe?"

"Maybe. So, people will still be out and about. I want to try something, but later. Closer to the twelfth hour when evening meal starts."

We wait until ample time passes and the outside light starts to fade. I put my mouth dead center of the hole, draw in a deep breath, and yell.

"*Tweeeeet-tweeeeet-kola-kola-tweet-tweet-kola-tweeeeet.*" Perhaps Uzi, with his big, pointy, floppy ears, is in hearing range and free to move.

"What are you doing?" Ahi whispers.

"I am calling my donkey, Uzi, so *shh.*"

"Oh, help us, Yahu. Help us."

No reply. I try again and hear the familiar response faintly.

"*Tweeeeet-tweeeeet-kola-kola-tweet-tweet-kola-tweeeeet.*" We cry at the same time. Uzi is here. His nose covers the hole.

"Good boy, good boy, Uzi. Love you, boy. Ifrah. Go find Ifrah. Bring her here." His nose stays at the hole. "Go now, Uzi. Ifrah. Find Ifrah." The nose vanishes. Shortly, our signal sounds.

"*Tweeeeet-tweeeeet-kola-kola-tweet-tweet-kola-tweeeeet.*"

"Aby?"

"Yes, Ifrah, I'm in here."

"Oh my god! I've been looking for you. What happened? Where are you?"

"Find something to make the hole bigger." She does. As soon as Ahi's face hits the evening air, she faints. Ifrah, Nimtsa, Seth, and Uzi drag her out and under the oak trees. I crawl out after her.

"My god, Aby, when I didn't see you or Uzi after three days, I thought you were back in Ramah or in Karmil with Moh. Nabal swore to it to me," Ifrah says with one part compassion and three parts anger. "Bentah hadn't seen you, either. And where was Uzi? What's going on?"

"I know, Ifrah. Lots of questions to answer but first let's get help for her. She is Ahi, wife number three." Ifrah clasps her hands to her cheeks.

"Can we trust the healer?" I ask and she nods. "Good. Go get her." The oaks are a good cover. The healer arrives with her arsenal of cures, and she is not alone.

"Moh?" We ask in chorus.

"Word came from Ifrah that you were missing, Aby, so I came back tonight to see what was going on. And Shlishi?

"Don't worry," Ahi starts. "I'm not sick or contagious. My color is disappearing and that's why Massa had me thrown into the cistern. And please call me 'Ahi' from now on."

"I am so sorry that this happened to you, ah, Ahi and Aby." Moh's dark face is flush with red as his eyes water. "I should have known and taken the right action."

"We know you would have, Moh," I say. "And we appreciate you for that. The important thing now is determining what to do next."

"I'm going to kick Zahra's ass," Ahi proclaims. "That's what I'm going to do next, as soon as the sky stops spinning." She lies back down on the ground.

"We should get you both back to your homes where Bentah can care for you," Ifrah suggests. "Then, we can meet with Nabal and Zahra and come to some kind of understanding."

"You cannot reason with a fool," Moh says. "Besides, what happens if Massa calls for you, seeing you milling about as normal."

"He won't ask for me," Ahi says. "Given my spotted skin. So, let us make spots on Aby, then he won't ask for her either."

"No," I ponder. "It will scare folks into thinking of plagues which could lead to our being stoned to death. That's too dangerous."

"Said the girl who arranged her own most useful betrothal and ended up here," Ahi jokes.

"For a good, even if rash, reason," I concede.

"I'm glad you're being more thoughtful," Moh says.

"What if we stayed in the cavern?"

"What?" Ifrah exclaims. "You can't do that, Aby. Look at Ahi now. She won't survive it."

"Massa, Zahra, and a few others already believe that we are confined or dead there. Everyone else assumes that we are away, visiting family. We can continue their confidence in either scenario."

"Like a ruse?" Moh asks with a grin.

"A ruse," I confirm.

"I like it," Ahi chimes in. "We could flood the cavern and make them think that we are dead."

"Might they look for the bodies?" Ifrah asks.

"Probably," Moh says. "The high priest will certainly want answers."

"That won't work, but we can go back into the cavern and live there." I say. "Hide our newly found entrance and exit in this oak tree grove and come and go as we please.

When we're out, we would have to go unnoticed. At the same time, though, no one would be looking for us, right?"

"Right," they say.

"Ahi," I continue with a wink to her. "This is how we become free of dead weight. We create a convincing abode underground as captives and find ways to usurp the king and queen of Kalebtu. The middle betwixt both is where we find our joy."

"The cistern, huh?"

"The cistern," I echo back to Ahi. "Where I can plot to save children without interruption and you can refashion it as our hiding place in all your spotted splendor."

"Let's do it," she laughs. "But after I whip Zahra's butt."

"I understand, sister, but that'll have to wait."

Ahi and I spend a few days at the healer's house to get strong. She and Ifrah concoct a special paste for Ahi to use to conceal the pale spots on her skin.

"This is not to hide your leopard-like complexion which I just love," Ifrah says when demonstrating to Ahi how to apply the brown clay-like cream. "Nor is it a cure because it needs not a cure. And it's certainly not a cause for shame, you hear me?" Ahi bobs her head. "This is to keep you safe and sane from the ugliness of people who can't yet see beauty in all things. Even themselves, for that matter." She lets out a belly laugh. "What I have here is a skin-deep solution for a skin-deep issue."

Before he returns to Karmil, Moh engages Lami-Yaj to secretly construct a concealed opening to the cavern that also offers clear visibility to the top ground.

Ahi sneaks in and out of Zahra's house to plant bugs, reptiles, and arachnids to scare her and her handmaidens. She was itching to do something.

Ifrah, Seth, and Nimtsa visit Abbah and Emah in Ramah to share what's happening in Kalebtu and assure them of my safety.

We learn that it is Tabbaha, the cook, who drops water and other sustenance into the cistern. Being none the wiser, she continues to do so. Bentah and a few other souls loyal to Moh and Ahi are privy to our scheme and hold our trust as they, too, see benefits for themselves. We decide it's best to keep our plan hidden from Pai, given her innocent inclination to Zahra.

I hide out with Uzi as much as is possible and safe to do as we may be apart for a while. Ahi and I gather all sorts of garments, housewares, food items, and cooking tools, and happily go into our hiding place.

CHAPTER 15

BENT

[be-int]: determined to do or have.

IN THE SECRET OF UNDERGROUND PASSAGES, oak trees, and disguise, I am planning the Bet Tsur development with Lami-Yaj when Ifrah comes into his office.

"Oh, ah, hello, Aby." Ifrah's wide eyes dart back and forth between me and Lami-Yaj. "I didn't know you were here."

"Hey. Yeah." We hug. "I'm delighted to say that Lami-Yaj is now the chief engineer for the sanctuary. And, we have connected with several producers, suppliers, and exporters to secure the materials we need to start construction."

"Wonderful."

"Indeed, Gebirah Ifrah," Lami-Yaj says. "How may I help you?"

"Oh, it's nothing. I, ah, just wanted to know—ah—had a question about the olives. I'll come back later, okay?"

"I will find you when we're done," Lami-Yaj counters.

With his long, bony fingers, Lami-Yaj makes a few updates to the designs for efficiency gains like rain capture and conservation ditches, underground water storage, earthen dams, irrigation systems, dryland farming, dry-stone fences, road access, agricultural installations, high adobe, and grass rooftops with chambers that direct wind through the home for natural indoor cooling, and waste treatments. Seth, who we learn is eight rather than my guess of five, is well-versed in math and helps Lami-Yaj calculate critical space and building measurements. I observe him from afar and he looks much healthier with fatter cheeks, brighter eyes, and a beaming smile, thanks, no doubt, to lots of Tabbaha's roasted barley bread and red lentil stew.

In between our tasks, I ask Lami-Yaj about his family, entry into Kalebtu, and prospects for his future. His use of words like "coercion" and "debt-bonded labor" disturbs me, so I persuade Ifrah to have similar conversations with most of the nearly three hundred adults living at Kalebtu who do not provide companionship or sex for Massa.

Many of them, like Lami-Yah, arrived here as indentured servants with Massa from his travels and trades in and outside of Kanaan. Whether seized to pay off a loan debt or sold by their kin for silver or some other money-related fix, Massa's negotiations usually ended up with the defendants in servitude to him. By Massa's crafty calculations and version of our debt cancellation laws, the debtors are rarely able to clear the obligation.

Some of the residents are newcomers who say they feel trapped. Others express feeling at home, having been here for ten or more earth revolutions, which is way past the six-year indebtedness time limitation dictated in Moshe's law, at least for fellow Ebres.

Several of the men wear an awl through a hole born in their left ear, indicating their choice for whatever reason to be a slave here forever. Massa takes some of the women for his physical pleasure. The few children here stay out of sight as Massa requires. Midwives are not allowed, a caution to those who dare consider birthing a child. Public awareness of a woman's menses is grounds for her being mocked on the palace lawn or even stoned, depending on whether Massa is full of strong wine. The hearts of most all Kalebtu citizenry desire liberty; others death. It's a disturbing imposition that Ebre Y'israelites know well. Perhaps, the people here are also fallen stars in need of sanctuary.

After weeks of hearing Ifrah's reports, I suggest a plan to Moh to free the servant-slaves and convert indentured labor into wage labor, giving them back some of their humanity.

"Go to Zahra. Take Pai with you and convince the first wife to champion the conversion as part of her queen's legacy to Kalebtu. She can present it to Massa, and it can honor them both. She will be known for making it happen and all Kalebtu will glorify her which is what she wants."

Ahi and I watch and listen from Moh's small office in the palace as the plan plays out.

"Peace," Zahra says as she greets the guard standing at the palace's front door dressed in ecru-colored headgear and robe. The setting sun casts a deep orangey ray upon him, making him look like a gigantic carrot. "I have a surprise gift for our lord, so he is not expecting me." She points behind her to the covered item held by Pai.

"Wait here," the carrot orders. A few moments pass before he returns to escort Zahra to where Massa, his top fool advisor, and two others are reclining against stacks of pillows, eating dates and grapes, and drinking from their goblets. Wine, I'm guessing.

"My lovely one!" Massa, appearing surprised, opens

his arms wide toward her but doesn't bother to stand. She bows slightly. "And my lovely two. I enjoyed you last night. You both look exceptionally enchanting this evening, which makes me happy, though I wasn't expecting either of you tonight nor tomorrow nor the next day. What brings you to me before your time? A gift, I understand, yes?"

"Yes, my lord," she starts. "Please forgive me for interrupting and coming to you unannounced, but I thought you might be interested in seeing this." She removes the shiny drape from over Pai's package to reveal a model of a monument to Massa. Pai places it on the meal table and stands back near the door.

"Ohh," he lights up.

"Yes," Zahra exclaims, clapping her hands in excitement. "We call it Bet Nabal. It will be a monument to greatness. Of course, it will be bigger. Much, much bigger."

"Oh, yes." He walks around it. "Incredible. How much bigger?"

"At least twice the size of the one for Melek Shaul in Karmil. You see this?" She points out the intricacies of the miniature statute of Massa in a long, flowing royal robe with a huge ring on his finger and a wreath of pistachio tree leaves on his head. Each word that she speaks evokes heightened glee from him. "This model is white, but the real statue will be golden to better glisten in the Kanaan sun. And the inscription on the top ribbon will read, 'Adon Nabal in his glorious triumph of freedom.'"

"I can't wait to see the actual statue and invite all my friends to see it too." He stares at it a moment more, then turns to her. "Freedom? Why freedom?"

"Now, Adon Nabal, there's no need to be modest.

What you're doing is grand. All the Ebre Y'israelite nation will be talking about it."

"Yes . . . well . . . of course they will," he fumbles. "What, ah, exactly do you think they will say?"

"Oh, they will call you brilliant. Grand. Fantastic. Great. Really smart." Zahra raises her hands to the sky. "Everyone will worship you more than they do now."

"They will?"

"Of course. Your amazing new decree is complete. Scribes are working this very moment to duplicate it for your announcement tomorrow at twilight when we observe the new moon."

He smirks and she continues slowly, "Yes, the—ah-ah, the—Nabal and Zahra Emer shel Darar."

"The what?"

"The Nabal and Zahra Emer shel Darar, a declaration of freedom that you are modeling straight from Kalebtu that turns bondsmen into share workers who produce more income than they do now for just a tiny portion given back to them."

"What?"

"It's a magnificent scheme and you will be remembered among gods for building your enormous empire by turning indifferent, sullen, and rebellious slaves—both our brothers and the strangers among us—into motivated and trusted people devoted to produce for you. The same way that Abbah Moshe stood up to free our ancestors from forced labor, so will you do, being forward-thinking enough to let them go. By releasing those in your servitude in a more benevolent way, you will entice them to stay with you and apply their skills in construction, weaving, metal-working, farming, masonry, carpentry, and other essential capabilities for your benefit and a little bit of theirs."

"So, the people stay here, working for me," Nabal ponders the idea.

"Yes, for the most part."

"And do the same work that they're doing now."

"Yes, for the most part."

"But I must pay them to do it."

"Only a little—just enough to mark their freedom and encourage them to increase their production and quality. And be loyal to stay and keep working."

"Exactly what would be this just-enough pay?"

"It would be a different barter for each worker. For example, I think that I heard you say recently at a new moon feast that you will happily give Tabbaha her own slice of land for farming if she'd only cook her famous wild lentil and lamb stew for you every day. With that land, she could make the stew and other meals for you and sell it to others, providing a portion of the profit back to you without any worry of sabotage. See?"

He nods hesitantly. "Or I could just keep her as a slave and punish her if she interrupted the business, and I could keep all the profits." The natural bent of Massa's greed starts bubbling up.

"Yes, you could, but that would make for a short institution with a high probability of damaged goods and angry workers who are forever looking to abandon or kill you, only leaving bodies scattered about the estate. Where is the shrewdness in that? How long would you trust eating that stew? With the Nabal and Zahra Emer shel Darar, you become the trailblazer, the boldest of lords, a true ruler for all the world to see." He sits up higher as Zahra continues.

"So, I will see to the pay details and, of course, they will favor you. I am also handling tomorrow's event so there's no bother for you. You can see out that window and hear how happily folk are already preparing for the celebration. And I expect all your friends and well-wishers will be in attendance."

Massa turns his head toward the window where the temporary stage is being erected though I doubt that he can see much from his short height and his seat on the floor. He thinks about her words while eating and drinking. She stands there like a tree.

"Let it be done, then, with one request."

"And that is?"

"Dance for me." He does not fail to reap ecstasies from most female encounters. It's the way he commands it with lust that makes my skin crawl. "You can still dance, yes?"

Massa claps his hands and young musicians enter the room. He and his goons laugh and take big swigs of wine from insignia goblets, apparently toasting Massa's ingenuity to convert slave workers. Zahra starts to move and Pai exits the house.

"Congratulations," Moh whispers to Ahi and me.

"Thanks to you," I reply. "They are all free."

CHAPTER 16

BEHOOVES

[bey-HOO-veez]: it is a duty for someone to do something.

"GOOD MORNING," HAILS ONE OF TWO ladies, kicking up dust as she hurries toward the weaving house to create exquisitely patterned and colored garments, tapestries, hangings, and other similar goods to merchants.

"Great rising," says the other, passing by me quickly.

I nod my greeting to keep my secret intact. Theirs is among a few new businesses springing up from Kalebtu since Zahra convinced Massa three moons ago to use share workers instead of bondsmen and formally organize the artisan activity here. Mainly, weaving, carpentry, and beading. Production is up and at a higher quality. Twenty percent of sales goes back to the workers, which most of them use to buy their own home goods and clothing. Before, they received nothing.

It feels like ten earth revolutions have occurred since those few days I spent with Dawit in Ramah. It's only been a little over two, and with help from friends, I've managed to keep my treasured virginity intact. My heart aches, thinking about our time together. I want to tell him about

Moh, Ahi, and Bet Tsur. I cannot. It's too dangerous for him with Shaul still hunting to kill him and likewise for me, being in hiding myself.

I keep busy, secretly helping Kalebtu residents, developing the sanctuary, and teaching three young people the sling so that they can help rescue child abuse victims and ready them for Bet Tsur.

Many nights, residents find food and goods left at their doorsteps or windows—gifts from my and Ahi's new business of redistributing Massa's wealth to the poor. In doing so, we often watch Massa from nearby hiding places.

"Sheeeeeeni," the voice calls out from behind Pai, spewing the smell of wine into the air. Massa and the goons following him are already drunk early in the day. Pai slows down.

"Sheni, my shweet, shweet Sheennnnnni."

"My lord," she answers. "I see that you've already begun celebrating even before the sun sets for sabbath."

"Not sho much and never mind it. I shhhee more little people 'round here than normal and think that it's because of you. Why are they here?"

"Me? No, my lord. I do not know. Perhaps, they are helping to produce the textiles and the jewelry and the woodworking?"

"They don'tsh belongs shhhhere. Runnin' 'round. Making noise. In the way. Eating too much. Hanging on dere momas. Taking my attention. Kalebtu is no place for 'em."

"Yes, my lord. I hear you."

"It bessshooves you to get da little rats out of shhhere 'fore I send them schhhattering off my shhhelf." He brushes past her. "And ifs I do, dere won't like it. Won't like it at all."

We hasten the Bet Tsur plans, already in development.

"You'll be at the sabbath meal tonight?" Lami-Yaj's eyes twinkle while he files away our paperwork, pleased with the Bet Tsur progress.

"Wouldn't miss it. I'll dress up like a weaver who most folks fail to notice." He nods. "I especially want to see the new products. Why do you ask?"

"Just wondering where you'll be," he smiles. "That's all."

"I will be unseen."

Just after twilight, Ahi and I walk behind the weavers to the palace's backcourt, near the food house. The smell of spicy lentil stew warms me before we even get there. The chatter seems higher and the lights brighter as folk congregate on the lawn. We pray and sing before filling our bellies with the evening meal.

"Greetings, Adon Nabal and everyone," Lami-Yaj says as he rises to the back palace porch where Massa sits. "I am delighted that we can break bread together again. Thank you, Adon Nabal, for allowing me this opportunity to speak. You are a most gracious lord. Please accept this gift as a sign of my gratitude." He offers Massa a pair of goat-skin shoes dyed the color of hyacinths blue, stamped with gold ravens, and tied with black rope. Massa accepts them with his head tilted back and his chest expanded. The crowd *oohs* and *aahs*, expressing their approval.

"I am pleased to announce," Lami-Yaj continues, tearing up, "that, thanks to our lord, my life changes for the better tonight." He reaches out to Ifrah, and she joins him upfront. "Ifrah has consented to betrothal with me. Nimtsa has consented to be my daughter. Seth has consented to be our son. And tonight, we enter covenant and become a family." Lami-Yaj can hardly finish his sentence when the rest of us clap and cheer with all our might. Nimtsa and Seth walk onto the porch, though away from Massa. The local priest comes forward and performs their brief ritual. A formal consummation is not required. With Seth and Nimtsa already their children and the fact that they've known one another already, doing so would be deception and none of us needs more of that so rounds of shouting and dancing commence with joy. It dies abruptly when Zahra walks up to the porch.

"As first wife of Nabal and, thus, your queen, I have an even grander announcement," she starts. A wave of fear washes over the gathering. "Thanks to our wonderful Adon Nabal, I am with child." A few people clap. Most are unsure how to react to living with the seed of those two.

"You said you're what?" Massa stands.

"I am with child," she pants and smiles with bright eyes. "We're having a baby and I pray for a son."

He stands, drops his head and starts to walk into the palace. "I am the lord and I say that children are not welcomed in Kalebtu."

Zahra starts to quiver in her sobs. Her handmaidens come to her aide and walk her down to her house. The party is over.

"What a beast," Ahi says as we walk toward the weaving house to keep up appearances. "I'd be afraid of that baby, too, but he should be thrilled to create another demon like him."

"No. He wants the glory all to himself and everyone else be damned, including his pregnant wife, even if she is as evil as he."

In three days, Lami-Yaj, Ifrah, Seth, and Nimtsa pack their things to relocate south of the salty sea, two weeks sooner than originally planned. Four other couples join them, comprising the founding villagers of Bet Tsur.

I am happy to follow them three weeks later with Moh, Ahi, seven fallen stars we rescued and hid over the past six moons, two nursemaids, four workmen, and three loads of Kalebtu-made products in tow.

The sanctuary's defensive wall greets us before our caravan gets there, causing my heart to burst with joy. Lami-Yaj opens the tall metal and wooden front gate to let us in. Twelve large tents form a half circle with the rock masses, which seem to reach to the sky, watching over them. Water streaming from the mountains serenade us. My dream, coming to light.

"Welcome," Ifrah waves to us, running and skipping. She and the other women stop cooking outside one of the tents to greet us with hugs. The men do the same, pausing their work to join the reunion.

"I have news," Ifrah says as she clasps my arm with hers and ushers me and the other women to our tents.

"You're with child, yes?"

"No. I don't think so."

"Okay. Then what's your news?"

"We learned two days ago that Dawit is in Ein Gedi, up the coastline from here."

"Is he?"

"Yes. He and his men are taking refuge in a cave north of the city."

"How do you know this?"

"Lami-Yaj and two other men were near Masud fetching supplies and heard about it from one of the sellers."

"How safe is he if tradesmen know where he is."

"They are not Ebres so I don't think they care," she ponders. "Anyway, it may be worth it to you to make a visit."

"Why is that?"

"Please, do not be coy with me. I know you."

"You do, and I'd love to go."

Over the next ten days, we work hard to build out the sanctuary. Plant more trees. Expand the vegetable garden. Build mud houses. Better secure the well. Construct water irrigation and storage. And enjoy good food and fun fellowship among loving people where children can thrive.

It's still dark and quiet in the morning when I climb the majestic hill behind the not-yet-dry village wall to a cliff that juts out toward the sea. The stillness I crave is hard to pin down. My mind scatters with wonder about Dah's hideout in a nearby town. *Is he safe? How long will he be there? Does he miss me like I miss him?* I exhale a sigh of defeat, arise from my spot, and walk back to our makeshift home to start my day's activities sooner than I thought.

"Back already?" Moh is checking the well's structure for what seems to be the one hundredth time. "The sun's barely up."

"Yeah. I had a tough time silencing the revelry in my mind."

"That doesn't sound like you." Ahi is coming from the cooking tent.

"I know. Ifrah's news of Dah keeps twirling in my head. That Shaul's men are still hunting him. That he's sheltering in caves outside a nearby city. That many diverse people know his whereabouts which means that Shaul will soon know, if he doesn't know already."

Empathy rises in Moh's eyes as I recount Ifrah's news. "Have you ever been there? To Ein Gedi?"

"A few times. I went for Massa to get dates, spices, saps, and other goodies. Only the best for him, you know."

"I haven't been there, but I've heard about its vibrant markets, lush gardens, and fresh springs."

"I hope to go back simply to enjoy more of its beauty. And if you must hide out, it's a good place to do it. Hills backed by big mountains on its west side. A network of crooks and crannies to disappear into."

"I haven't been there either," Ahi says. "So, let's go."

Her suggestion meets silence. "Well, it is on our way back to Kalebtu," I finally say.

"It is closer to Ma'on than here," Ahi adds. "And Moh, you already know how to get there."

"No," Moh says.

"And if Dah just got there, then Shaul may not be there yet," I advocate.

"No," Moh says again.

"We could help him," I continue.

"Really?" Moh is doubtful. "What could we possibly do that the hundreds of men with him cannot?"

"Well, well . . ."

"We could . . ." Ahi takes over. "We could be scouts for him on this side of Ein Gedi and report what we learn to his men."

"Are you out of your mind?" Moh looks at us as if we both just grew another head. "This is, with all due respect, an Aby-crazy idea—ideas I thought you were no longer entertaining. Besides, I must be back in Kalebtu in two days to start preparations for the shearing season. Without me, it's a hard 'no' for you two."

"Why is that?" I am unmoved. "We can't go on our own?"

"What?" Moh laughs at the thought. "What is this? Has the old you returned?"

"No. No, I'm thinking this through with you."

"You cannot go without a male escort."

"It's on the way to and just a short distance from Kalebtu. And it may be the last chance I have to see Dawit again."

"There is too much warfare, thievery, and abductions around and about Kanaan for women to go roaming miles on their own."

"You know well that I can handle myself with the sling." I raise my weapon.

"And I am precise with the bow." Ahi points to her bow and quiver already hanging on her back.

"Plus, we'll have Uzi and he's as smart and tough as any man." My smile is met with Moh's frown.

"And if I say 'no' a third time?"

"Then, we won't go," I concede, even though Ahi and I both outrank Moh on the authority scale. "But this is a low-risk, short-term detour on our way back."

"Seemingly." Moh throws up his hands, indicating his own concession, even if unhappily so. We leap lightly toward him with hugs and smiling eyes. "I can't believe I'm giving in to this." He pauses and pushes back from us, his hands to his face. "So, the Y'israelite–P'lishtim feud has died down for now. That's good for you two. And Shaul is only looking to harm Dawit. I will go with you part of the way, then tell you a straightway to get there. To address the last issue I have with this, you both will have to agree with an inflexible requirement."

"Anything," I say. "Just name it."

"Go as young men."

We spend the rest of the day finishing our community tasks. At sundown, we have our last supper at Bet Tsur, for now, enjoying a simple yet delicious meal of bread, honey, lentils, and figs while sitting around the fire pit beneath the backdrop of lit candles and a heavenly mountain.

"Dodah," I say, having a warm chat with Ifrah at the pit. "I've been watching you. You seem quite happy."

"I am. I was not the sister—aunt to you—who desired marriage or children, but here I am. Full of joy and peace with Lami-Yaj and our growing family. Everyone is happy in Bet Tsur. The energy is good here. Already, the other ladies and I have discussed the seven children you brought and which ones we each want to mother. We plan to start a school to train the children in all sorts of skills. Everyone here agrees that we can create some sort of product from the sea to sell at marketplaces to support the community. And the herb garden, Aby. The herb garden." She claps her hands to her mouth. "My apologies. I'm going on and on about your project. When I start talking about it, it's hard for me to stop."

"It's not my project."

"Huh?"

"I realize at this moment that Bet Tsur is no longer my project. It's yours. And Lami-Yaj's. And all the others here. I will forever be committed to rescuing abused children, but I see now that the establishment of this community and its future belongs to you, Ifrah."

She is silent, twiddling her fingers. "It behooves me to agree, and I would be honored to do so, my sister-niece."

"That brings me joy." We hug and hold one another before the long day and the night air nudges me back to my tent. Sleep evades me and I toss and turn, unable to get Dah off my mind so I arise in the deep night. Ahi is already awake, staring at me.

"Your sleep, if you want to call it that, was like a live performance. Your body was darting left and right and rustling like a trapped jackal. I couldn't sleep."

"So sorry, Ahi. I didn't mean to keep you up."

"You're going to see Dawit today, so what's wrong?"

"I don't know but I kept having disturbing visions. A dove, flying into the sun. Dah, standing in a fiery tree. Me being torn from my children. Omens, you think? I mean, are we doing the right thing going to Ein Gedi?"

"You want to see him, right? A lot of people will be around, so you won't be alone with him, right? And he probably won't even know you're there since you'll be there as a man, remember?

"Oh yeah." We giggle.

"Come on. You'll feel better after we get ready."

CHAPTER 17

BEDARKEN

[be-DAR-ken]: to darken or *obscure.*

AHI AND I QUIETLY RATTLE AROUND, packing our things as the rest of the villagers slowly emerge. Our tents will stay as housing for future residents and visitors. We meet Ifrah at the wash bowls where she has laid out a couple of sheep-colored tunics with ritual fringes, top mantles, colorful scarves, bulky sandals, and chunky jewelry she got from her husband and the other men.

She rubs wet charcoal around our lips and along our jawlines to mimic beard stubble, then ties the scarves around our heads to make turbans that cover our hair, foreheads, and mouths. Lami-Yaj inspects her work. He decides to punch small holes in our tunics to allow more airflow and lessen the buildup of heat so that we, as he puts it, don't die by the sun on the way. We dust our hands and feet with dirt and sand to make them look more rugged and then practice gruff voices that mimic Eber Y'israelite men. Ahi goes to present her new self to Moh and help him pack the donkeys.

"You love Dawit," Ifrah says to me with the sternness

of her sisters. "You even desire him. I get that, trust me. But don't let that bedarken your eyes to how this world works and cause irreparable harm to you and to him. Understand what I'm saying?"

"I think so," I murmur.

"Consider what will happen to you if the two of you are found in an improper way. And to Dawit, with Shaul salivating for any reason to end his life. Be very careful."

"I will, Dodah," I hug her tightly. "I will."

We leave Bet Tsur at first glimpse of the sun, going north along the salt-brushed sandy shoreline banded with black mud. Bold songbirds glide above, I think, to cheer us on.

"Here is where we split up," Moh says when we make our second rest stop, this time at Masud. "I will turn west and go up to Ma'on. You two continue north along the shore until you get to green grassy fields, towering palms, the sounds of people and cattle, and the smell of citrus fruit. Then, turn east up through one of two big canyons and you'll come out on the edge of the town. Go eastward and start to look for Dawit's camp somewhere in a cave north of the city. You should get there with plenty of daylight to find safe shelter in case you don't locate him. Kalebtu is straight east of Ein Gedi. Have yourselves back there before dark tomorrow or I must come looking for you and I won't be happy about it. Got it?"

"Got it," we confirm and wave our goodbyes, being too bulky to hug.

We journey as Moh instructed. The left side of our salty trail soon widens into a dirt path which later gives way to blankets of green and orange foliage, giving us a foretaste of the lush haven to appear.

"You hear that?" Ahi whispers with part thrill, part

alarm, compelling a nod from me. We stop to view the looming oasis like drips of honey just shy of a toddler's reach. To our right, white-spotted brown fallow deer munch on plants of a bushy pistachio tree. *Perhaps, the noise we heard?* In the distance, two flows of water cascade from deep-orange, limestone cliffs into springs below, and the sweet fragrance of henna blossoms and balsam trees float in the air, inviting us forward.

"We're close." I prod Uzi east and up a narrow gorge.

The gorge suddenly opens to a grove of many tall date palm trees and hefty fragrant shrubs that surround a multitude of clay buildings and tents built on rocky hillsides and flat plateaus. Various vegetable and fruit gardens and vineyards grow behind the structures.

We enter and weave ourselves through the grove, going north. An assortment of people—tradesmen, nomads, artisans, shepherds, royals, slaves, priests, sex workers, rich, poor, beggars, thieves—busy themselves among the marketplace exchanges, workplaces, food houses, and sleep lodges. At the northern point of the city, we exit right from the palm grove into a scattering of cottonwood trees that lead up to the edges of the surrounding mountains.

"Take another step." The growl of the voice in my ear is deep and serious yet strangely familiar. It pairs well with the rock-hard stomach pressed against my back and the bear-like arm gripping my neck, all sending a paralyzing bolt of fear up my spine. "Do it, please, and I'll rip this little pulsating artery so that your red blood spews artistically on the gray gravel." That voice, I'm sure, belongs to Raddai, Dah's blood brother. "Turn around slowly." He has his hand axe already cocked back. I also see the silver ram cylinder high up on his ear. "Who are you and what is your business here? May the mighty Yahu strike me down should I not end your life right here if you do not answer well."

"I-I—" My mouth, like the rest of my body, is as still as the stone altars of our deity. I clear my throat, remembering my deep, manly voice. "I am here seeking the one called Raddai, son of Yeshi."

"What need do you have of him?"

"I was told by my kin in Ramah to ask for him to do what is right and join up with the honorable one, Dawit, also son of Yeshi."

"I am that Raddai, and we have no need of runts like you who get themselves killed and whose blood ends up on our hands."

"I am well-skilled in the sling, my lord, and an excellent rider."

"I will be judge of that." He looks around the area. "You see that row of pomegranate trees behind that hut? Hit the last one and knock down a piece of fruit. I'll let you know whether you have skill or not."

Verve returns to me in the face of his challenge. I pull down my sling, load a stone, and start my wind up as Raddai raises his axe again. Just before my release, I whistle. *Whack! Crack!* The tree swings and the fruit breaks into pieces. My gut tightens with joy, and I turn around to see fright in Raddai's eyes.

"Abyga'el?" He grabs my arm and tears the turban off my head. "Aby! What the hell!"

"Ah, ah, ah."

"What are you doing here?" He moves into my face. "And why are you violating our law by acting and dressing like a man? I could have killed you and then my soul would be in danger."

"I—ah—we came to help Dah and you and the others."

"We?" Raddai looks around.

Ahi eases out of the bushes on my right side, causing Raddai to jump and raise his axe once more.

"Ra, this is Ahinoam. Ahi, this is Raddai, Dawit's brother."

"Another woman?" Ra squats to the ground. "Have you both lost your righteous minds? You could've been killed or worse!"

"Mmm, not sure what's worse than being killed, but okay," Ahi attempts to ease the tension.

"There are worse things and be glad that you don't know them." Ra, not laughing nor smiling, turns back to me. "You're a helluva long way from Ramah but you can't stay here. I'll tell you how to ge—"

"We have traveled so far. Please, please don't turn us away. Take us with you so I can at least see Dah and know for myself how he's doing and if there's anything I may do to help him. And we will leave tomorrow. I promise."

"Damn it, Aby. How am I supposed to explain the two of you?"

"We are simply two of Dah's many admirers who want to do our part for the cause, to keep him safe from Shaul. That's all."

"How would you intend to do that?"

"I don't know. The same way you do, I guess. Scout. Signal. Scream. We'll stay in the background and cause no trouble to anyone."

"And say nothing?" He stands there, shaking his head and thumping his foot.

"Nothing." I reset my turban as best I can.

Raddai takes a deep breath and holsters his axe on his hip. "You see that ridge up there? That's where we're going. Follow me. Step where I step because getting there is better suited for wild goats and I don't want you falling off a cliff, leaving me to have to explain that disaster. You, nor her." He glares at Ahi, still in her disguise. "And when we get to the camp, you both keep your mouths shut. And I mean shut!"

We walk along a rock-cut path around and down the side of a hill, moving at the pace of Raddai's long strides. Shelves of earthy red and dark orangey limestone greet our steps as craggy cliffs jut out overhead and disguise small doorways to underground hollows, deep chasms, and bedarkened caves. Wild, dense jujube trees dig their hardy roots into rocks and yield their prickly branches as home to honeybees that deter intruders. We slosh across a stream of water trickling lightly through a drying riverbed, muddying our steps. A herd of horned Nubian rams stop their nimble hike down a grassy hillside to evaluate our sneak past them while two wild rabbits spring from a crevice in the earth.

Ahead of us, shepherds dressed in white clothing huddle under tents near stick-fenced sheep pens at the cliff's summit just above a waterfall, no doubt cooling off from watching their herds in the summer heat. After Raddai greets and chats with them, we leave Uzi and Ahi's donkey in their care and walk a bit farther. Far from the eyes and ears of the Ein Gedi town, I take a chance on violating my oath of silence.

"How long have you all been here?" I ask in a whisper, staying as small as I can.

"That is not keeping your mouth shut."

"I was just wondering whe—"

Raddai takes about fifty more steps before moaning his frustration. "Three moons."

"Is it safe?"

"Safe enough. We've managed so far by the mercies of Yahu and the many hiding places in the wilderness and among the caves." The thought puts a smile in Raddai's voice. "Shaul's army has a base in the city where they make merriment at night. They'd rather not try the rocky places in the dark."

"But you do?"

"Yes, ma'am. I'm a ram that's like a desert fox. I can roam around here at night with no problem." This time he laughs out loud. "I wouldn't suggest it for you, though. We know how to do it, sleeping in one of many caves at night and during the day when Shaul's men are hunting us, we spread out and blend in with the many shepherds, providing them protection from, you know, bad guys."

"And Shaul's men don't notice you."

"Nope. We know how and when to go unnoticed."

"Nice." I feel safe.

"Oh," Raddai slips off the cylinder from his ear and amulet from around his neck and hands them to me. "One for each of you. Put them on so we don't kill you by accident."

We do, and our little party returns to silence for less than a half mile, feeling our way on or under one rock ledge or flat outcrop to another, until we come midway of a hill where an overhang to the right of cascading water hides a rough triangle-shaped opening, about twice my height and width.

"*Coo, cooooooooooooo, coo, coo,*" Raddai calls out and receives back a similar dove-like sound with a slightly different pattern. "Go," he says to Ahi and me. "And remember, don't say anything."

Lowering sunlight lands just inside the entryway where we step into the long, glorious atrium of a cave.

Ascending walls and arched ceilings of chalky stone, marbleized in browns, creams, and gray greet us. The cooler air eases the discomfort of my hot, itchy costume. Near the back of the atrium stands a man, likely Raddai's fellow coo-er, who holds a lit oil lamp. He nods at Ra, and we follow him through one of two corridors. Dawit is standing in the center of this much larger and even cooler area. The electrical currents within me start brewing up my spine again. I guess about one hundred men are with him, packing up their camp and removing signs of their habitation.

"What is happening?" Raddai's question bounces off the walls. "What are we doing?"

"We're going deeper into the cave, away from the opening," a husky man answers with a deep voice that doesn't bounce as much. "Now that more of Shaul's men are in Ein Gedi, they are bolder to venture out after sundown and into this area. We've got to see or hear them coming before they see or hear us."

Ahi and I trail them as they descend the cave by oil lamps. Five men stay behind as watchers. None of them seem bothered by our presence, likely because we came in with Raddai. We walk through a passageway that circles to the right before landing in another spacious cavern. Its location appears to be underneath the entrance room. I still hear the flowing water. A gentle, warm breeze sweeping across my face tells me that we are not too far from another opening of some kind.

"Tuviyahu," a young, thick man calls to another as he re-twists his locs and ties them into a single braid with a strip of blue linen cloth.

"Yeah, man," a slender, slightly older man with golden skin answers. "You need me, bruh?"

"I need you to tell me when your wife's sister will be ready to wed and bed. I would be a better man with a tasty little thing like her by my side."

"It would take a lot more than her to make you a better man," Tuviyahu hoots. "You couldn't even pass her father's brutal what-can-you-do-for-me test."

"You did."

"Look at me." He stands, turns around, and flexes his muscles. "I am a god. I can pass anything. Don't chase what I do because you could get hurt." The room roars with laughter, and I thank Yahu that we are outside the hearing range of those hunting Dah. Hunting us.

Ahi and I are privy to such banter for two more hours over dinner of raisins, dates, olives, flatbread, and water in the dimmest of light. Dah leans back in a nook in the back of his new home, eyes closed, and tranquil, like he did in Gan Aby. I stroll near there, pretending to serve food and drink to my fellow warriors, and hear him mumbling in prayer.

"Great Yahu, hear me, as you always do, and have mercy on me, on us," he says. "Though my enemy hounds me to vex my spirit, you refresh me and watch over my way. I find shelter in your ever-presence, even when facing lions and voracious beasts in a dry and parched land, knowing that even this challenge will benefit me. So, comfort even my pursuer who is higher than I. Free me to emulate you and your ways, so both the righteous and evildoers will see your goodness and know that you are the true and living creator."

Let it be done as he has said. His plea is tangible and his humility is alluring.

"Dawit is sensuous and magnetic," Ahi says when I get back to our side of the chamber. "More than I imagined he would be. I like it."

She giggles and gets back to rearranging her bag until we find it necessary to go with Raddai to the other side of this lower part of the cave to relieve ourselves and freshen up our disguises. He is a protective and honorable guard, and we will owe him our first-born children, if we get through this night. Some of the others tease him about our being his devotees, but he waves it off as trainee attachment, like they once had for Dawit. We laugh it off and resume eating or talking or sleeping, until we hear heavy footsteps topside followed by another cooing signal.

Dah raises his right hand and dead silence sweeps over the camp. The already low lamps go immediately black. Dah creeps out of the room, taking a left back up the corridor. Ozem and Ra follow him. My heart beats loudly in my ears as I sit motionless on the hard, cool floor. The frozen, wide-eyed stare on Ahi's face makes me signal her to breathe so that she doesn't pass out. We wait, staring at one another and struggling to hear what's happening above. The one named Tuviyahu walks to the door of the cavern. A few of us join him, sneaking up the lower corridor, easing our way into the first hiding room, and crawling just inside the passageway that leads to the atrium.

Dah, O, and Ra are crouched on the ground at the other end of our hiding place, just before the atrium, seemingly in a hot debate over something. We can't tell from here. A majestic man with long, thick locs and height like a tree is standing near the cave's entrance at the waterfall with his back to us. His statue is obvious, causing my stomach to leap. *Melek Shaul. In Dawit's refuge cave.*

The king is alone and unarmed, relieving himself. We slink up the passageway as Dah and his companions slip into the atrium and hide behind large rock columns. Dah sneaks stealthily close enough to Shaul to kill him but instead slices off the right edge of the royal robe dropped at Shaul's feet. Dah slithers back to his hiding place and rests his back on the big boulder. A scowl covers his face.

When Shaul leaves the cave, Dah jumps up and runs after him.

"My king," the boom of Dah's voice rouses the tranquil night. Hyenas retort with their pitched *whoop-whoop* howl. When Shaul turns around, Dah is bent down on the flat hillock with both hands lifted, showing his reverence for the king. All is silent as everyone else watches like statues that do not speak or move.

"Dawit?" Shaul yells out in a startled voice. "Is it you?"

"Truly, my father. It is me." Dah rises with his hands still raised. "I call to you in sorrow, wondering what I have done to offend you so gravely. Why do you listen to the voices of strangers who say that I aim to harm you, that I am no longer your son? This is not the case."

"Is it not?"

"Of all the caverns in this desert, Yahu led you into the cave where I slept. I was so close to you that I cut off this corner of your royal robe. Do you see?" Dawit holds up the cloth, crumpled up by his tight grip. "I could have easily killed you, but I did not. Why? Because you are my king, anointed by the great Yahu. My heart grieves at the very thought of harming even a hair on your body, of even defacing your reign by my act tonight. It was wrong of me to do so, and I ask your forgiveness. I will not raise my hand against you but will only protect and honor and respect you as a son of Yahu. As am I. As we are, which makes us brothers.

"Why, then, are you so bent on taking my life? Am I less than human to you, like a dead dog or a nasty flea? What has the king of Y'israel to fear? What did you come here to do, evil or good? May Yahu judge each of us and our intent, and thus defend me to you. Let this fringe be a witness for me that I am innocent of any crime against you."

"You are right, my son," Shaul yells out and begins to cry. "You are more righteous than I because I have repaid your faithfulness and goodness with sheer evil."

Shaul is repenting? I doubt it. All of the night remains deathly silent as he continues.

"You could have returned evil to me this day as Yahu delivered me into your hands, yet you did not. You chose the blameless way and I pray that the great one rewards you with equal good for that choice. I now know for sure that you will be king, and that the kingdom of Eber Y'israel will rest and rise in your hands. Swear now to me by Yahu that you will be as you are now and show mercy to spare my sons after me and not erase my name from Bet Kish, my father."

"Let it be as you have said," Dah sounds relieved. "Fear will not bedarken my heart."

Shaul leaves with his awaiting men, hopefully to go back to Gibeah.

"You should have killed him and put a quick end to our persecution," Raddai argues quietly.

"No, that is not our way, brother." Dah puts his hands on Ra's neck, looking him eye to eye. "No harm will come to Shaul by my hands, by our hands." Ra yields grudgingly.

The rest of us go back into the cave with surging joy and jubilation. No one died today and, maybe, Shaul's pursuit of Dawit is over.

Dah makes an altar to Yahu of small stones just inside

the cave and calls it Derekh Yahu El Hofesh, meaning the way of Yahu, my god, is freedom.

A celebration of drink, music, and dancing starts instinctively, and I sway with it.

"Stop it," Ahi scolds, reminding me of our ruse as male trainees. I slump back toward her, frustrated that I can't celebrate in earnest with Dah yet my heart sings that I'm so near him and get to watch his gratitude in full, flagrant motion. We stay lowkey in the back of the atrium, fading into the limestone to protect our identities and enjoy the festivities before finally falling asleep behind one of the big rocks.

CHAPTER 18

BENEDICTION

[ben-e-'dik-shun]: short blessing concluding a matter.

"HEY." RA KICKS MY FOOT. "Get up. Time to go."

"Already?" The sun has not yet made its way into the cave. "It's still dark."

"And? Get up."

Others are milling about. Packing, eating, relieving themselves, and talking about the encounter with Shaul. A messenger of Dah's rushes into the cave and heads down to its lower level. Minutes later, I hear Dah shouting commands to his troop leaders, his voice drawing closer. Activity in the cave swirls swiftly, like ants pouring out in attack mode when a human steps on their home.

"Ozem, good, you're dressed. Go now to the pen with five others. Prepare the mules and wait for me there. Eliyahu, you and Ubu have the rest of the men finish closing camp here and then go southwest to the mountains in Pharan where we were before. It should be safe there now." Dah finally emerges into the atrium, still putting on his outer garments and weaponry. "Sham. Qeren. You two go ahead of me to Ramah. Ra and I will be right behind you with the others."

Ramah?

"Excuse me, my lord," I say in my gruff voice. "What is happening? What can we do?"

"Do as you are told. My father, our high priest, is ill and I must go to him. Hear and heed your instructions. Follow your leader and you will be safe."

Though his words are slow to enter my ears, they shoot straight to my stomach and give it a hard punch. Ahi and I grab our things and run after him and out into a blue dawn, fastening our weapons as we go.

"My lord. My lord," I holler in my most manly voice. "May we accompany you?" I'm going either way, but I prefer to ride with them. I pray he grants my request. "We can assist with the—ah-ah—goods and the animals and any needed tents."

Dah turns around and looks me up and down. "From where did you come? Did you join us in the wilderness of Ma'on?"

"Well, yes, something like that."

"I'll vow for this one, Dah," Raddai interjects. "Let them come and let's hurry to Ramah."

Dah is still staring at me when he says directly, "Keep up."

They move at a fast pace with swords and stones clinking rhythmically with every gallop and trot. Ahi and I huff and puff to keep up. By the time we stop near the town of Bet Lekhem, more than our halfway point, both Uzi and I are sweaty and breathless. We welcome the rest. Ahi stares at me openmouthed as if she is seeing my ghost. Charcoal streaks cover my lower face and drip onto my manly tunic. Hers is doing likewise. My head covering, poorly fixed by my own hand, is unwrapped and spread across my and Uzi's backs, leaving my hair flipping and flopping in the sun.

"Abyga'el?" Ozem is the second to notice, causing the others to look at me. "Is that you, Aby?"

"Aby?" Dah comes near, looking into my eyes and seemingly desires to touch me as I do him. "When did you . . . why are you . . . what are you doing here?"

"I-I-I—" My thoughts escape me, and I am speechless.

"It's a long story," Raddai rescues me again, tapping Dah on his leg. "I'll tell you about it later. Let's move on."

We ride hard and make the journey in half the typical time, arriving before the third hour when the sun is not yet high.

"Please attend to our mules," Dah instructs one of his men, though he and I hardly stop for our dismounts before we jet to the inner court.

"I'll send word to Moh," Ahi yells.

I run beside Dah around the community building, into our house, and into the hallway of the high priest's lodge.

"Whoa, whoa, whoa." The dutiful Noach stops us. "Aby? Why are you dressed this way? It is not permitted for you to wear men's attire, and you know this."

"I—"

"It was my doing," Dah answers. "It was to protect her and the other woman with us as we rode here with enemies, bandits, and such roaming about. I thought it best that way, for their sake and ours."

Noach seems satisfied. "You can change quickly over there where robes are hanging behind that screen, and please be calm. The high priest is resting. I know you want to see him, and he wants to see you, but compose yourself and prepare for a peaceful visit."

He's right. My appearance alone of tousled hair,

sweaty face, and men's attire would be upsetting. The pause gives me a moment to be still and breathe, if only for a second. I change my garments, refresh my face and lips, and cage my thick, curly tresses into a blue satin scarf. *Much better.*

We slip into the sleeping room where Abbah is sitting on his hewn bench with his back against the wall. A large, linen cover rests over his legs. Emah is tinkering with cups and pots and tea leaves at a table on the other side of the room. Abiyah sits on the floor and Noach leans against the wall.

"You're here," Emah says, smiling and hugging us both. "And together." She stares at me. "It's at a good time. He is stronger during the day than the night."

I ease down in front of him on the bench. "Abbah," I whisper, taking his hand in mine. He looks his handsome self. Strong and composed. Bright smile. White cottony beard rivaling his brown leathery face full of friendly lines and twists. I'm grateful for that. His eyes, though, herald other news. Enlarged pupils. Glassy and a little watery.

"Aby," he struggles. "Dah. My daughter. My son. You're here."

"Of course, we're here. Where else would we be? What I want to know is why you're testing us so with this silly and annoying tease of leaving this realm? You are not going anywhere, are you?"

"Here, drink this." Abbah takes the tea that Emah offers. "It'll help with your breathing since you're determined to talk now that Aby and Dawit are here."

"My body may be going indeed, my dear," Abbah says more strongly and clearly after drinking the tea. "But fret not. This exit comes as my friend because my experiences are full and complete."

"No, Abbah, no," I cry.

"Hush, child, and celebrate with me. I have lived a good life in this form, and I have no regrets. Not one. I loved and have been loved. I governed my people with vigor and justice. I rejoiced in having a righteous wife and vibrant children. I did all that Yahu directed me to do and I am ready to go." He looks at Dah. "Now, it's your turn."

"My turn? Old man, you must hold that mantle longer, at least until the crazy man stops hunting me, and who knows when that will happen." Dah forces an unconvincing smile.

"Help me to the window."

"Shmuel, no," Emah issues a strong command, stronger than I've ever heard her use with Abbah before. "Don't give in to stiff-necked pride. You should not exert the energy to stand up."

"Woman, do you not see? Do you not know? This is my last sermon to you and to them. Let me have it, please." Emah sinks back, tearing up. Now, it's Abbah who's in search of a smile as he stands up wobbly, knocking his knees, and holding on to Dah's arm as he walks.

"Come," Abbah calls to me. "I want you to see this too."

"Yes, Abbah, what is it?"

"There, way in the distance, is the tip top of our cherished tent of tabernacle, our place of spiritual meeting." He gazes off into the distance with fascination, like a high-flying fowl eyeing her river prey. Yet, nothing is there. The fifteen-foot high tent in Gibeah isn't visible from here, not by the physical eye. "Yet, I was in the spirit three days ago as I began my ascension back to Yahu and learned that the tabernacle tent is not the true dwelling of Yahu." His eyes grow full of water and his body starts to shake slightly. "It is what I need you to know."

"Worry not, Abbah," Dah says, helping the old man back onto the bench. He sits up higher, sips more of Emah's warm brew, and takes a deep breath. I massage his arms which are cool to the touch. "You have already given us everything we need to know, not leaving anything out."

"No, my son. There is more. Things I never considered before. Things not taught to me but are for you to advance." He pauses with concern on his face, allowing me to wipe away his tears. Others are wiping away their own.

"When we are not at the tent for appointed times," Abbah continues now more composed, "where does Yahu dwell? In the tent? No. The great energy is in you whether you're in the tent or not. I recognize now that this is what's been maturing in me ever since that day as a child, I responded to Yahu's call which was as clear as a full moon."

"My lord, that should be enough, yes?" Emah pats his right hand and Abbah lovingly pats hers back yet continues his lecture.

"Though the body's flesh and bones represent your earth as a magnificent outer court that interacts with the physical world, it is only a shell of the true you. Like the tabernacle, the ephod, and the two gems. As beautiful and symbolic as they are, they are worthless if we do not see them as pointers to the truth of what is occurring within your own mind, heart, and spirit as the true inner court, the secret place, the holy of holies point of connection to Yahu that neither slumbers nor sleeps. It is always on, always open, always accessible, always listening, and always answering.

"You, as the high priest of your own thought, will, and decisions, examine your minds. Is it for good, life, and blessings, or the absence of that? You get to decide. But know that whatever you choose is what you will experience in this realm. It is Yahu's law that works within the dark of your deep mind and heart to create what eventually comes to the light, even if you know it not, and nothing can change it. So, choose well. Choose life, blessings, and peace—just as you would if you were picking ripe, luscious pomegranates from a grove." Abbah pauses once more to again restore his breath and drink more from his cup.

"Abbah, we hear you," I say in the room's silence. "We know your heart, so you no longer need to speak it. Simply rest."

"I know. I'm taking up too much of your time but on—"

"No, no, that's not what I meant." I sigh. "We're here for whatever you want to do or say."

"This I will leave with you as my final benediction. Rejoice and be glad because nothing emerges in your seen world unless it first be sown in the unseen ground inside of you. You are the operative mystery of creation."

What does that mean? He bows to each of us, then points to a dark wooden chest with a big latch sitting in the corner of the floor which Noach and Tetteh carry to him.

"My son," Abbah raises a large package to Dah who steps close and takes it. "I pass this to you and all that it implies for now and the future. You will need it as you take the weight of our people's righteousness on your shoulders and until you trust in your atonement with Yahu from within." As tears stream down his cheeks, Dah unties the package to find folded inside a short, intricate linen tunic of gold, blue, purple, and red threads, and a square gold shell divided into twelve gold squares, each holding a precious stone. Abbah's priestly vestment. His ephod, waistband, and breastplate.

"Yahu has said it. You shall be king. Also, be priest. Let them know that Yahu is in Eber Y'israel through you.

Return her heart back to Yahu and rule her well. Show Shaul to be the example of what not to do." Abbah lays his hand on Dah's head. "May Yahu bless you and keep you and expand you. May Yahu hasten your pace and empower your understanding, so you no longer have need of outside objects. And always go in peace."

"My daughter," he turns to me.

"Oh, Abbah." Adoration, gratitude, and sorrow swell up in me at once and I start to sob into his leg, dampening his garment. "I-I love . . ."

"Hush now and look at me," he says, and I do. "Fortitude and vigor were upon you when I first saw you, even as you slept. They only grew stronger with your age and even birthed impatience, which I hope you'll work on." He beckons Emah and she comes with a small box. He opens it and pulls out the gold-chained amulet containing the prayer that his predecessor gave him.

"Here," he chokes out. I rise on my knees, so he easily puts the chain over my head. "I allot this to you as a reminder to be and live you, knowing that Yahu will light your path." He manages a smile as he places my hand in Dah's. Sparks fly up my spine again, despite the occasion. Dah weaves his fingers between mine, and I feel safe. Protected. Comforted. "Love conspires to find a way for the two to become one.

"My love to you all," he addresses the room with a fading voice. "This is not a time of sadness, but joy. Death is nothing, only the shedding of this outer court. The true me, my inner court, will remain in holy unity with Yahu and, as such, a part of the Yahu within you. I will be with you always."

"Let us allow our beloved to rest for a while." Noach gently helps Abbah to his bed, signaling us to say our goodbyes and exit the room. Once out, I press my back against the wall across from Abbah's bedroom. The warm, hard, and coarse plaster pricks my skin, distractingly so, making it easier for me to hold myself together. Dah has his own space on the opposite wall.

"This can't be happening," I say tearfully.

"I know," he replies and comes over to hug me, his touch and soft voice in my ear igniting again that fiery bomb inside me. "He will be fine. We will be fine." He pulls me off the wall, puts his arm around my shoulders, and steers me to the food house for sustenance. Even as the little bit of energy I have left oozes out of my body, my heart rate rises, and my breath deepens just being this close to him. We wash our faces and hands outside the door before entering. Thoughtful sadness permeates the place. Even Tiye is refraining from activity. No one asks about my home in Ma'on or brings up Nabal. Butterflies swirl around the growls in my stomach so I only drink water and a little goat milk. Dah pops figs into his mouth, one after another out of hunger or nervousness. I'm guessing the latter, but glad that one of us can eat.

"What were you doing in En Gedi?" Dah asks, shifting our minds off Abbah. I knew the question was coming.

"Looking for you." I try to read his face, but he is stoic.

"Why?"

"To see how I could help you and, well, to see you again."

"That was a dangerously dumb and unnecessary thing to do. It's a long ride from Ramah to En Gedi especially during times of war and more especially for women. I had plenty of men with me."

"I was told so."

"You should have listened to Abbah or Emah or whoever told you."

"Then we would not have seen one another or been together."

"We didn't see one another, and we weren't together. You were a man. Another dumb thing to do."

"I was not a man," I giggle. "I was dressed as a man to make the dumb thing not so dumb."

"Really? It didn't work."

"It did. We got there safely, and you nor the others detected us."

"Ra evidently did."

"Yeah, that. Our one little mistake. He crept up behind us just inside the skimpy forest edge, you know, beyond the town. I was scared witless and sure we would be killed right then and there. My body turned into stew when I heard his voice."

"You should have never come there at all, and especially not way from here." Dah shakes his head, finally permitting a small smile. "Again, dumb, and I'll certainly deal with Ra for letting it go on."

"I'm sure," I say quickly, wanting to end the topic and dodge the fact that I no longer live in Ramah. "Hey, I see you're holding fast to your vow not to kill our tarnished king."

"I wasn't kidding when I said so. I have no trouble killing, when necessary, but this one is not my place, not my doing. Otherwise, I could have killed him already."

"Could you believe that he was in the cave and alone?"

"I was stunned."

"It could have gone terribly wrong at any moment."

"I never want that, even if he does."

"I was proud of how you handled it."

"Mmm. I hope he sticks to what he said and gets his good sense back because I've had enough of being a fugitive for no good reason."

"Hopefully, he is too, and is enormously grateful that you're an honorable man who didn't kill him then and there."

He looks at me, remembering something. "Oh, and as I've told you before, whenever you need me, simply send a messenger and I will come here to you. Don't go roaming around trying to find me. Promise?"

"Promise." We sit there awhile, picking at the various victuals on the table. "What do you think of what Abbah just shared? He said, 'You are the operative mystery of creation'?"

"Interesting, for sure. I spoke to you a little about it when we were last here and upon the wall." He points to our night spot so many moons ago. "The things Shmuel has often talked about with me seem out of this world or beyond our time, so what he just taught is another example of that. I've done some things that others see as impossible so—"

"Like the giant."

"Maybe. But more so, not killing Shaul who is clearly trying to kill me. Either way, my ability to do it doesn't come from outside of me. It comes from inside of me. A sort of internal guide that is me, but much more than me. Yahu and me, perhaps. So sure, I can accept that I am— each of us are—a worker of that one great energy. That is why I go to it before I do anything. So, yeah, I get what Abbah was saying, and I hope that it works that way."

"Shall we go back?" Not only do I want to be with Abbah, but I can give Emah a break. Just as we walk into the sunlight, blasts of the ram's horns ring out. Three broken sounds followed by one long, loud note. Death. A ripple of wails from near Abbah's quarters. A dove, flying into the sun.

Dah yells out and tears his tunic. I tremble to the ground. We weep, finding ourselves in need of benediction as our joy vanishes like a jumpy desert hare fleeing into a narrow hole to elude a golden-eyed jackal that swiftly comes at night to devour it.

CHAPTER 19

BEREFT

[be-reft]: deprived of or lacking (something).

SHMUEL IS DEAD AND NOW WALKS among our ancestors.

News of his death spreads quickly. Soon friends, relatives, and members of the Eber Y'israelite nation start to show up in Ramah. I watch them pitch their tents in nearby fields and arrange their personal items, many planning to be here for seven days of mourning. They start doing certain things that must be done in certain ways to pay due respect to the high priest and the last judge of the Ebers.

Priests adorned in black consecrate residents and sympathizers at the courtyard altar. They also ignite incense burners at the entranceway, throughout the village, and along the dirt path to a burial cave hewed out of the side of a higher hill behind the village where Abbah's body will be laid to rest.

Twenty-four elderly, barefoot women, cloaked from head to toe in black goat haircloth, flank the inside of Ramah's front gate. Not needing this time to pull from their repertoire of laments or even require pay, they begin their vocal songs of sorrow and commence the sounds of our shared grief. Subdued chants and groans. Dull hymns. Soon, their eyes puff up and turn bloodshot while sweat pours from their brows. Drummers thump on timbrels, providing a steady beat for our relentless tears as dancers rise, sink, shake, swing, twist, and turn to dry them.

Spectators join them at the gate. Some are dressed in their own black clothes or have their tunics torn, often with dirt and ashes on their foreheads. Most keep their hair and lips covered while the locs and faces and feet of others go bare. Some fashion shaven heads or clipped beards or even gashed bodies, following their own minds or native rites as such bodily desecration for the dead is forbidden by our law. Some folks are given strong drink made of blue lotus flower water and wine to calm their hysteria, while others refuse food altogether. A few people curl up in a ball upon the ground with their loins girded with sackcloth, fixed in their vows of silent prayer.

I walk to my room slowly, passing Abbah's private bathhouse. I know what is happening in there. Sights, sounds, and smells confirm it. A male servant goes inside, carrying a basket of linen cloths and strips. Noach and Dah mutter familiar chants and sacred texts as they do what women typically do: cleanse Abbah's body with warm hyssop water, anoint it with oils of balsam and myrrh, and wrap it fully in linen strips, preparing its swift and welcoming return to earth. As they do, an assembly of priests chant and pray outside all along the front of the house.

I quicken my steps and go back to my room to remember Abbah in solitude. I sit on the floor barefoot, take a deep breath, and go into the silence with tears streaming down my face. Peace is there. Warmth. And Abbah, smiling at me.

"Why do you lament, my daughter?" His voice is soft and calm. "I am not dead. I have simply transitioned to another form."

"I should have been there," I whimper.

"Nonsense. We enter this realm alone and exit alone. Before and after, we exist. I said this to you, did I not? Arise and rejoice! Be you. Live you. I am with you always."

The voice dissolves into tranquility as quickly as it came. And I feel him now. Unmistakably, his spirit swaddles me long and hard. It is warm, comforting, and empowering, and snaps me back to being me. A better me. I dress in my own bereavement black. Each layer of the lightweight linen goes on like steel, dense and cold. I welcome the dark and full coverage that hides my private and personal recovery.

Emah and I walk with Abiyah and his family to the front gate full of folks. My brother, Yo'el, is not here. He left Ramah and swore never to return after Abbah severely reprimanded him and Abiyah for being dishonorable judges before Y'israel got a king. They had begun to rule wickedly, taking money to decide outcomes. Abiyah came back several years ago and made amends. I guess Yo'el is holding to his promise.

Many people reach out to touch our arms or shoulders or hands; others simply cry louder into their napkins as we walk by. We stop at the wooden, railed funeral bier covered with a large, multicolored shroud on which Abbah's corpse rests. It lies there wrapped in a beige, linen, spice-laced winding sheet with the high priest's linen robe and a prayer shawl draped over it from the waist down. Only his face is uncovered, still conveying peace and purity. The body is alone without familiar grave offerings. No food, no garments, no trinkets, no talents—as Abbah taught. "The body is material and, at death, immaterial," he would say. "The spirit needs no accompaniments, status, nor wealth to go back home."

Twelve student priests, six on each side of the bier, hoist the platform upon their shoulders and carry it out to the road, just outside the front gate. Bearers of our tribal signs, one for each of our nation's twelve tribes, are already lined up there. They each hold up the mark of their father's house stamped on large tin squares mounted on a pole. Both groups wait quietly for the procession to the burial to form.

The wailing women follow the bier, accompanied by the musicians. Noach and all the other priests follow them. Next is Shaul in his formal, dark-blue robe that drags the ground and reflects the shimmering light. Some folk bend low to the ruler, others do not. One of his sons, four royal courtiers, and a stocky army commander gird him. Massa walks with him, frowning occasionally at me. My stomach turns, not from seeing Massa again. I know how to evade him here. I worry because Dah is also here, though I haven't seen or heard from him since the final dressing earlier today. He and his crew may be using the crowds and their tents or even another cave to stay in Ramah unnoticed. *But for how long?*

After Shaul is Emah, Abiyah, and me with Moh, Ahi, Gullah, Ifrah, and Lama-Yaj. Behind us are thousands of people adorned in their own darkness and ash. We start the mile-long walk, moving several abreast like black ants following the scent of their leader until we reach the shallow but wide valley between Ramah's back wall and the upper northeast hills of the village. There, in the faint of dusk, thousands more people are gathered, lighting more lamps, and thronging the flats and crevices all over the hills.

Some six yards overhead is the now well-lit walkable ledge to the cave tomb's door. An inscription above it reads

"B'nei Elkanah." Sons of my grandfather. The large, stone slab to the right of the entrance stands guard like a sentry awaiting its next order. The student priests place Shmuel's body on a stone bench in the tomb, then line themselves against the hill's wall on both sides of the cave opening.

A half-moon slowly takes its place over the horizon and the bereft congregation quiets itself when Noach appears at the front of the ledge and taps his staff three times, sending an echo into the valley like thunder.

"Yahu has given, and Yahu has taken," he starts. The acoustics of the hills in the cooler evening air take his voice with clarity to every listening ear. "Blessed be the ways of Yahu forever and ever."

He unrolls the writings of Moshe that Abbah used, reads a short portion from it, calls upon Yahu to comfort his people, welcomes all those gathered, and confirms the solemn occasion. One of the wailing women calls up a chant and almost everyone answers her.

Father Abrah'm!
He is in the light.
Father Yitzak!
He is in the light.
Father Yaacob!
He is in the light.
Father Moshe!
He is in the light.
Now, Father Shmuel.
He is in the light.
Is he in the light?
Yes, he is in the light.
Yes, he is in the light.
Yes, he is in the light.

As Noach raises his hands to hush the cries of the congregants and begin the eulogy, a trumpet sounds and Shaul rises to the front of the ledge, now with ashes all over his uncovered hefty locs. He no longer looks his robust self, but rather shaken and weak yet he nods to Noach to step aside. Nabal stands directly behind him. *Idiot.* I move slowly and farther behind Emah and out of his line of sight, expecting to stay as far away from him as possible.

"Fathers, mothers, brothers, and sisters," Shaul begins. "It is I, Shaul, son of Kish of Binyamin, servant of Yahu, and the king of Y'israel. Your king." About half the crowd claps, because of love or fear, but Shaul keeps going. "I bring you comfort in our time of great distress for the days of our great prophet Shmuel, son of Elkanah, son of Yeroham, son of Elihu, son of Tohu, are over. We, the sons of Y'israel, have suffered a great, great loss." Shaul pauses to wipe tears from his eyes. "We are now without our leader, our loving father, our advisor, our ... solace ... our ... light." He starts to sob almost uncontrollably, prompting Nabal to rush to the king's side, whispering in his ear and compelling the barefoot women to wail again.

Could he genuinely be distraught? I doubt it. Emah says that the last time Shaul saw Abbah was nearly fifteen years ago. That was the day Shaul confessed that he had defied Yahu's directive to destroy all the Amalekites in war as retribution for wickedly ambushing and attacking our people without cause centuries earlier. Instead, Shaul kept alive Agag, the Amalekite king, and their best livestock for sacrifice. Samuel relayed to Shaul that his rebellious and reckless choices had caused Yahu to reject him and replace him as king of Y'israel. Shmuel corrected the king's misstep by killing Agag and never saw Shaul again. His tears today may be more about regret than grief.

"Yes, this is our darkness." A calmer and more controlled Shaul continues with his arms outstretched. "But do fret not, my beloved. The future of righteous judgment within our nation is intact. Our high priest did not leave us bereft of hope for he taught me well. You already know my military prowess. I led the defeat of many of our formidable foes, including the P'lishtim. And when our beloved was unavailable and in his fashion, of course, I led critical sacrifices to Yahu according to our custom. A righteous king and priest, like our notable forefather Melchisedech, who does everything, and I mean everything, to benefit the Eber Y'israelite people. This very night, by my power and orders, watchmen are about you, searching for any evildoers among us, even as we lay our beloved to rest. And contrary to ugly rumors, Yahu remains with me to guide me as your king and to empower me over my enemies, both near and far. That way, we can re—"

Shaul is doing what he does best: milking the occasion for as much bragging as he can get, and I have had enough. I back guardedly and quietly from the front of the crowd toward my place of comfort at the village's back wall.

"I know you're not buying that crap." Hands squeeze my shoulders firmly from behind me, ending my exodus. A familiar voice whispers in my ear. Dawit. "That makes just a few of us."

"My Ash."

"No, don't turn around." The pressure on my shoulders swells in a good way, making me wish that his hands were on a few other places of my body. "I'm the evildoer and enemy he's talking about and it's only a matter of time before he is back on the hunt for me. I'm leaving now but wanted to see you, touch you, before I go."

My womanhood melts at his words, yet I maintain my composure and shift my head so he may hear my murmur. "Where will you go?"

"Back south," he replies and Ein Gedi pops into my mind. "I will mourn in Pharan. Stay strong. Be watchful. I will come back to check on you and Emah as soon as it's safe."

"But what if we ge—" My muted words are futile. The hands are gone. He's gone, leaving a tinge of his intoxicating scent. I get back to my family just as the tomb is being closed and Shaul enacts his final public display of sadness, sobbing without comfort. Other than that, the burial is done.

I welcome Moh and Ahi to my private perch atop the village wall. Though the day has been long spent, we are still alert and chatty. How? I do not know. So, we watch the people. Public woe steadily turns into a celebration honoring Abbah. People leave flowers and personal trinkets at the grave as they dance their way back into the village. Some stay in the valley, singing and dancing and touching one another amongst lit lamps as musicians play. Others gladly cook and clean as an expression of their self-appointed duty to serve the bereaving family with the cup of consolation during this lawful time of mourning.

"Look," Moh points to a scene behind the wall. "Over there." On the east back of the valley, near the hillside, and to the right of a boulder, are the shapes of three men. The big, bulky one looks around as the quite tall, slender one changes from his long, smooth, shiny robe to a scraggly, animal-skinned one with a hood. Shaul and his beefy commander enter the forest, followed by the short third man. *Massa.*

CHAPTER 20

BEWITCHERY

[bi-'wi-che-re]: a magical method
meant to initiate an outcome on or for someone.

WE SHIMMY DOWN MY COVERT PEGS on the wall, muscle through the crowd to get outside the village gate, take the left-side path to the back valley, and sneak into the forest. Though the darkness is dense, a starlit sky gives an inkling of light that helps us avoid injuries from stumbling over tree roots or stepping in holes or some other night-hike-in-the-woods catastrophe. Our clandestine follows the three silhouettes over a dome-shaped mound and down a tiny hill until they stop in a dirt clearing. We do likewise, just before the opening. I climb quietly to the mid-limb of the terebinth tree and wrap myself around it like a snake. Moh and Ahi crouch like iguanas behind two extraordinary stumps of felled oaks.

A fourth person is already in the open area, placing on the ground a large pot crafted of shimmering cooper and decorated with giant, winged, gold beetles all around it. *I've seen that vessel before.* A stack of broad fig leaves and a slender, clay jug sits near a noticeable rock behind the worker whose movements suggest a female. Next to them are two birds. A white dove softly coos and an ebony raven gutturally croaks, each in its own tiny, wired cage.

"My lord." The doer greets Shaul, confirming her gender. She is covered from head to toe with only a sliver of her eyes showing which muffles her voice.

"My priestess," Shaul replies as the woman stoops down and starts to draw on the ground. Two eyes, one horizontal and one vertical. They overlap at the eyes' centers where the pot sits. The corners of the eyes create a four-pointed star, perhaps a point for each physical force of fire, air, water, and earth, plus the middle circle that represents spirit? Or, the four directions of north, south, east, and west? Or the four seasons of spring, summer, fall, and winter?

"It seems that we are here again," Shaul continues without any response from the worker who is now putting letters at each point and along the lines of the dirt eyes, but I can't make them out. I don't know what this is. But what I do know is that this same star design, along with ravens, is on the monument for Shaul in Karmil and on the clay pots around the palace in Kalebtu. And that this woman is a witch. "Your king is in need of your wisdom and unique gift of making close contact and agreements and arrangements with the sacred powers and mysteries." He begins to walk around the glade, observing the witch's work and convincing us watchers to remain utterly still.

"Of course, we wouldn't be here had Nabal succeeded with the plan and had our beloved not died so soon."

What? I gape at Moh who gapes back at me and rests his right hand on his chest, gesturing for me to stay calm as the witch fills the pot with a thick oil and what looks like water.

"I did everything you told me to do," Massa answers without concern.

"It was a truly brilliant idea," Shaul continues as if he's speaking to himself, ignoring Massa. "Tempt the child to marry the fool with the land she desired for whatever crazy reason she had. Then, coerce the priest to make wrong his prophecy, put me back in good graces with Yahu, and reinstate the beautiful and apt union of king and priest that we so enjoyed. It would have secured the longevity of my kingdom. All the fool had to do was exploit the well-being of his new wife to stronghold the high priest. Mild warfare. Royal captivity. But Nabal—alas, his name is exact—corrupted his assignment with stupidity and death had its own plans for the priest."

Nabal's threat to Abbah at the wedding. One of the goons clipping my fingertip. Zahra cutting my hair. Only Yahu knows what else. Shaul, Nabal, and the witch, maneuvering me all along and testing my father. I want to pull my sling and kill all of them right now, but I didn't bring my weapon. Besides, rash behavior is what got me in this predicament, bringing innocent Abbah with me. I won't make that mistake again so I undo my rage, watch, listen, and long for Dah. He would know what to do if he was here.

"It was not my fault," Nabal screams. The watchman steps to him and he sits down on a nearby boulder.

"Now Shmuel is gone," Shaul persists, still wandering the dell aimlessly. "With him, I fear, are my hopes for atonement at a time when my biggest threat, Dawit, remains allusive. The P'lishtim are quiet, but for how long? What do I do? I must know what measure to take." He stops his pacing and turns to look at the witch, who stands in front of the now-burning pot with a dove in her right hand and a knife in her left. "Get to it."

She cuts the throat of the dove, sending blood flowing into the vessel, and carefully places the bird's remains into the fiery pot, then lifts her head and outstretched arms to the sky. "*Ommm bah bah bah,*" she moans for a minute or so. "*Ommm bahhh. Ommm bah bah bah. Ommm bahhh.*

"I call to you Sachiel, great and holy prince of Yahu, full of mercy, covering, and strength. Be among us and hear my cry this night on behalf of your son, your servant king. Shaul is his name, son of Kish of the tribe of Binyamin. I am Gullah. I am Meira. I am darkness from whence comes light."

Gullah? The witch is Dodah Gullah? I at once recognize the sharply green balsamic bitter fragrance of galbanum. Her favorite.

"Whisper to the one true and all-consuming fire. Entreat it to incinerate the sins of your servant king and liberate him from his prison of error. Blot out from his page every sin and wrongdoing that stains and shames his name. Yes, my lord, do this, I pray, now so that the wrath of Yahu subsides and the dark stone upon your son's head dissolves. Walk across your compass, oh great angel, with your falcon eye. Set your son on a clear and straight path, one that will revive his mind and secure his kingdom. Be a helpful companion for his success, just as the sun lights the day and the moon brightens the night. *Ommm bah bah bah. Ommm bahhh.*"

She tosses two handfuls of torn fig leaves above the flames. A few of their chards pop and scatter over the sketched star. She slithers to the star's point where most of the pieces fell and kneels over them, her right forefinger skimming their outline.

"What do you see?"

"The shapes tossed from the flame show four distinct forms."

"Which ones?"

The witch bends forward closer to the leaves. "Cross sticks. Another eye, like the one I drew but without the star. A rope. And a doubled container."

"Doubled container? What does it mean?" Anxiety drips from Shaul's words.

"Okay, so, right to left, they reveal this as a sign, or my sign, that your twistedness is seen and now comes to an expected end."

"What?"

"Fear not, my lord, and hold on. Let me read the leaves the other way. Left to right. Remember that the message could be either way. This way, I see the boundary of the darkness or wickedness as limited or dead which is already seen or commanded by the divine powers. It is their sign or signal."

"Is that supposed to be better?" Shaul yells. "That's no better."

"There is still the libation which can rearrange the leaves or cast a new, more fortunate sign."

"Do everything that you can do."

Gullah snaps a jujube thorn from a tree scarily close to my hiding place then pricks Shaul's finger, pushing his blood droplets into the stationary jug. "*Ommm bah bah bah. Ommm bahhh.* Mighty and benevolent prince of the magnificent Yahu, I come once more, thanking you for hearing me and understanding the dilemma of your servant son. Attend to my pleas a second time. Withhold not your given power and authority to relieve sinners of their guilt and scorn. But allow your mercy to stir anew upon your charge as a fierce wind that brings his rebirth and a flourishing kingdom like this raven that soars to the heavens."

She sets free the other fowl and it flies away, escaping the knife.

"I feel your breath, fair and just prince, flowing now to revive your child. Yes, new wine in new wineskin being poured out for him as I pour this out for you." She picks up the jug and starts to dispense its liquid atop the charred leaves. Suddenly, a blade of fire stretches from under the searing pot like a furious sword and strikes and annihilates the mixture as a bright blue flame, blazing through Ramah's night sky, striking Nabal's left leg, and knocking Gullah backward. The smell of burnt flesh and fermented white grapes fills the air. The jug sails across the dell and smashes into a tree. It is a divine intervening and fitting finale to this disastrous ritual.

Shaul, his guard, and a staggering Nabal fade into the forest, leaving the witch on the ground. We watch as she crawls to the conspicuous rock, takes a deep breath, gathers up evidence of the ceremony in a large back sack, and walks back to the village. She is in the alleyway leading to her sleeping house inside Ramah's walls when I call out.

"Dodah Gullah." She stops and turns around slowly. "What have you done? What did you just do?"

"Whatever do you mean, my precious and grieving niece?"

"I was there. Tonight. In the clearing." Her jaw drops as her eyes turn cold. "And I heard all that you said and saw everything you did."

"Are you sure, little girl? Perhaps, your sorrow is causing you to hallucinate."

"As sure as I am standing before you right now."

"You know, children should stay out of grown folk's business."

"Who are you to say so? A royal harlot, trading your bewitchery for selfish schemes and manipulations. An inept sorceress who betrays her own family. A fool toying with the—"

"Don't you dare begin to tell me what I am," she yells and spits. "You-you-you naive ingrate who should be on your knees, thanking me for making you a rich woman. Had I not done what I did, you would have been married off to some commoner like your father was when Zellah married him, rest his religious soul. She may have ended up being the wife of the high priest, but as you saw I am the one our king faithfully relies on for mystical arts and curious workings. I am the royal diviner of Eber Y'israel. I am the one!"

"Is that it?" The fright in her eyes answers me immediately. "You concoct a plan to use me to torment Abbah into doing something that he would never, ever do as if I'm just a piece of bloody flesh to dangle before a hungry lion then throw out when it is no longer useful? All because you're still angry with your sister for being her father's favorite and for her getting betrothed before you, seven decades ago? How disgusting! You and your king may have finagled Nabal's proposal, but I was the one who accepted the offer, and I chose the fool for my own reasons.

"I was in awe of you when I last saw you, Dodah." Tears start to stream down my cheeks. "That was almost three years ago but no more. I am no longer that person so here is what you will do."

Gullah leaves Ramah in the dim of predawn amid others who are heading north. Like Yo'el, and as I requested, she swore never to return as she means Emah no good. I say her farewells and excuses to her sisters, who conclude with sadness that her oddity is due to envy and discord and is best left alone.

In three days, Moh and Ahi leave for Ma'on.

"There is much to do before the wool harvest," Moh reminds me. "So, I would best get to it before Massa does something stupid."

"Probably too late for that," Ahi says.

"I understand," I admit. "But Ahi can stay and be free of the cistern for a while longer."

"Then, who would relieve Massa of his fat pockets to share the wealth?" She laughs.

"There will just be more for us to spread around when we return."

"If we return," she wears an inquisitive smile.

"For the sanctuary's sake, I must return at some point," I answer her unsaid query. "The Bet Tsur land has been filed in my name, but is six moons away from being final, contingent as you know on my being married and alive three earth rotations.

"For the sanctuary then," Ahi raises her hands high into the sky. "I will with great joy remain here and return there with you."

"Glad you two worked that out," Moh jokes. "Feiwel will stay here with you. You know him, right?"

"Of course," I nod. "He helps us with the wealth redistribution."

"Oh, yeah," Moh continues. "He will stay in Ramah with you to accompany and support you, Emah, if needed, and will escort you back south when you're ready. He is as me, understand?"

"Yessir, my lord, we understand," Ahi and I giggle and Moh shrugs us off. Same shadow, different man. I smile again at the thought.

I spend the next seven days of mourning in quiet reflection with Emah and Ahi, followed by goodbyes to the dozen or so departing priests who extinguish the lamp left burning in Abbah's workroom. They announce that our sadness is now satisfied and, as command by Yahu, we may get back to normal. Things will never again be normal.

My grief lifts as the rains dry and summer arrives. Uzi and I take Ahi to Gan Aby, and she helps with village chores, getting to know Emah, Tiye and other Ramah residents. Emah convinces Ahi to exist without the skin cover up, which makes them both happy. I appreciate more the openness, uplifting, and shared purpose of the village community. Respect and pride. Treasured things that Abbah cultivated to help people thrive as individuals and as a group. Things that I took for granted. Nabal, Zahra, and the throw-aways taught me how wrong I was. Noach and Emah will lead them now. The folk here don't need me but those in Kalebtu do, so I will arise and go back there and, possibly in doing so, cross paths with Dah again. "*I will mourn in Pharan.*" That's what Dah said, so I will watch for him there.

CHAPTER 21

BÊTISE

[be-teez]: an act of stupidity.

EXCEPT FOR A FEW WATCHMEN, COOKS, and servant women, Kalebtu is a graveyard. Massa is at Har Mihamon in Karmil to shear his sheep, an occasion of celebrated excess. He demands that his household attend to help honor him and the abundance of his enterprise in a distinctive Nabal fashion. Ahi and I leisurely enjoy the quiet and pleasantly warm day repacking our sacks with the things we expect to need in Karmil before finally dawdling there.

Typical for this annual event, Massa's cherished gold and red banners embroidered with black ravens are visible from a distance. Prodded by a pleasant breeze, they fly high above the front gate, teasing and waving me into the wool harvest that's nearing sundown of its second day.

Har Mihamon glows as the playground for hundreds of Massa's friends, patrons, allies, hangers-on, and members of the royal house, if not the king himself. Mostly men. No elders sit at the gate. Any wise men who might be here are at the marketplace on the interior court under elaborate and colorful awnings to watch buyers haggle over the exchange of raw wool or sturdy textiles and to settle disputes among sheepherders and traders. That includes Moh who closely manages the entire shearing operation—from inspecting the first fruit of the wool to assessing its quality to recording expenses and profits and minimizing Massa's disregard for righteous dealings.

Two ornate tents, almost as large as Massa's two-story house, sit on either side of it as homes to high-ranking notables. They block our view of the festival's status but don't curtail the noise. We take the left path and walk past Shaul's monument where tribute flowers, charms, and other trinkets spread wider and stack higher than normal. They also provide back support for four men who are fast asleep. Mercy for them should Massa or Shaul catch this scene. A few children, whose parents apparently had no other option but to bring them here, push and chase wooden hoops on the lawn left of the statue. *May Yahu have mercy on them.*

Ample tents for co-wives and many other lovely huts and smaller tents for the rest of the partakers comprise a thick barrier behind Har Mihamon's permanent buildings and around the central inner courtyard. We weave through them beneath the many tall poles that each hold two lit lanterns until we reach mine. The entry curtain is closed, an oddity in this warm weather. I pull it back and find an overweight man with colorless skin and hair romping with four thin, nude women, dancing, jumping, and laughing around him and the silver shekels strewn on the woven rug.

"Go away." A woman with long, skinny, dark brown arms yells and rolls her eyes at me.

"No, beautiful, join us!" The man sits up and yells a lot louder and gruffier, spewing his breath, reeking of wine and musty cannabis smoke, past my nose.

"There is not space for another," the woman replies with a shout, hissing through her teeth.

"Excuse me, people," I say calmly. "This is my wife-of-the-host tent."

"Not anymore," she struts toward me and recloses the curtain.

"Aby?" Pai emerges from her abode next door. "Shlishi? Hello!" She greets us with tight hugs. "You two have been gone such a long time. Rishon said that you would not be with us for shearing."

"Yes, the prodigal wives have returned," Ahi says. "And please call me 'Ahi'."

"Oh, okay. Well, I'm just so glad you're back." Pai looks over my shoulder. "What's wrong? What's with the yelling?"

"A man who eats too much and the women of his harem who eat too little have made their wild abode in my tent."

"Oh, yes. That." She peeks through the curtain's slack. "Rishon allotted your tents to special guests. Shall I'll get them out?"

"Don't bother. I'm not surprised, and it suits me just fine to be off the front row. I'll get someone to hoist up our dwellings elsewhere, maybe behind the big weavers' shed where flowering oleander bushes with pink flowers will buffer the noisy, stinky revelry and offer a touch of privacy."

"Let's go this way." Pai directs our steps to the left of our tents, the long way around the central courtyard. "You do not want to see first wife just now."

"You're right, I don't," Ahi confirms. "But why do you say not?"

"That, well, seed inside of her has made her as harsh as Massa," Pai whispers. "It's like she spits fire."

"No doubt," I giggle. "Where is Moh?"

"He is doing what he does, you know? Probably wrapping up today's financial recordings in the operations house which, this season, is next to the first wife's tent. Going this way, we can stop to see him without crossing her tent."

"Good." We continue our trek. Pai expresses her sympathies about Abbah and my state of heart. I ask about her fitness and conjugal visits with Massa, which are minimal nowadays. We comfort and celebrate one another. A few people from Kalebtu stop to gawk or point at me, Ahi, or us both. We keep walking.

Various harvest activities congregate on our right in the vast patchy grass fields of the central court, encircled by the buildings and tents on our left. A low-to-the-ground performance stage creaks and cracks to the pulse of musicians, dancers, minstrels, and dubious prophets. At the food shelter are hearths and pots for outdoor cooking and stations that offer a multitude of food and drink. Guests stroll around with a shoulder-strapped bottle gourde, etched with Massa's signature ebony raven, that they fill at the food shelter with their drink of choice and a necklace made of artichoke heart and mint leaf pieces intended to lessen the effects of gluttony and liberal intake of beer and wine—things like stupor, spasms, incontinence, nausea, indecency, violence, depravity, and other betises.

Food, drink, and other hospitalities get replenished with supplies from Kalebtu to satisfy any appetite over the eight-day festival.

We notice Ibo. He is tallying up what he says is the next 250 sheep to be sheared, the first batch of the last one thousand to begin processing at dawn. They wait patiently in a big pen behind an airy barn where a legion of professional shearers—stinky, dirty, sweaty men skilled in and well-paid for their use of short, metal, spring-type hand shears—are cleaning up, putting away their tools, and washing themselves to close for the day. Others work fast to finish sorting, weighing, and bundling the wool for raw sale at the marketplace or delivery to the weavers. Ibo promises to have my new tent put up right away.

We continue around the perimeter of the court. Three teams of thirty-two women weavers in the tent beside the shearing barn work sunup to sundown in shifts to clean, treat, air, tease, dry, comb, and spin the wool into thread and then spectacular woven and dyed garments, tent covers, and other textiles. It makes for a constant output of goods sold during wool harvest at three and four times their normal prices. When they aren't working, the weavers usually eat, sleep, tend to their families, or go to men's tents for sex or whatever.

Moh is exiting the operations house when we get there. I hold to them tightly, pushing back tears of joy at seeing him.

"Glad to see you too," Moh beams to me and Ahi. "We will have to catch up later after I close out the marketplace." He cuts through the center court toward the weavers.

"So . . ." Zahra appears in the yard and pierces me with her reddened eyes. She waddles near us with her hands on the lower sway of her back, making her swollen belly look bigger than it is. "The seductive troublemaker from the pit has risen." She looks past me. "And with what I believe is your resurrected, diseased companion. I was sure that you two would starve to death while we all were at shearing. Disappointing. If you were as smart as they say you are, you would not be here. You would have stayed in the cavern and never showed your face again. Silly girl. I could have you caged right now, but I won't ruin this specular festival and moneymaking event for my husband. But as soon as our lord is done with his wool trading and back in Kalebtu, you'll know the pain of a thousand lashes or some other proper penalty for your disrespectful behavior." She grins, rubs her pouch, and turns to Ahi. "And that goes for you too."

"I didn't come back for Nabal and I sure as hell didn't come back for you."

"Why did you come?"

"Because the slaves you call friends, servants, and residents need liberation from the yoke of you and your husband so that they have a say over their own lives and futures. You know who will do it? Me."

"Over my dead body." She moves closer to me and the brown patches on her already dark cheeks, nose, and forehead stand out, confirming her maternal state, as if it was even necessary.

"Your choice." I lean in her direction despite the constraint of my friends.

"Let's go," Pai says as she and Ahi pull me back. "Let go now."

"Wake up," Ahi calls into my tent. It is way past sunrise and she and Moh came by to check on Uzi and me. "We haven't seen you. We haven't heard Zahra's mouth. So, our concern and curiosity brought us here."

"You two are like gold to me," I hop up, stretch, grab

my robe, and fluff my hair. "I can't believe that I slept so late."

"Yeah, especially when the bleating of the sheep almost right next to you is so loud," Moh jokes. "Maybe your snoring scared them."

"I do not snore. Loudly." We all laugh which is a delightful way to start my day.

"Truly, though," Moh calms his merriment. "Are you okay?"

"I got good rest and am much better this morning."

"You brought your betrothal veil?" Ahi touches the airy fabric.

"The long one."

"You're using it as the entrance to your tent?"

"I find that it works quite well for that. I have the shorter one, too, if I need it for extra screening. Thank you very much."

"You are odd."

"Why let it go to waste?" I say with all my sensibility. "It has to be good for something, right?"

"I can tell you what isn't good. That." Ahi points behind me where Ibo is bursting through the hedges and coming this way, his colorful coat flapping in the air. Moh turns around as Ibo stops just short of us, bending over and gasping for air. Basaka and Mushi, leaders on his sheepherding team, catch up to him and do likewise.

"Peace, Ibo," I say, looking between the three of them. "All is well?"

"No, Gebirah Aby. Gebirah Ahi." He takes a deep breath. "No, Moh."

"What is it?" Moh's eyebrows draw together, wrinkling his tightened forehead.

"We . . . are . . . in . . . very . . . big . . ." Mushi wheezes out, "trouble . . . this time."

"Why? What did you do?" Moh motions for them to sit and drink the water Ahi offers.

"Not us," Basaka answers. "The sheep farmer."

"Massa," Ibo clarifies.

"What bêtise did he commit now?" Moh exhales and rolls his shoulders back.

"He made an enemy of Dawit, son of Yishai."

"What? How?" I stand up.

"Dawit and hundreds of his followers have been in and out of the wilderness of Pharan for a while now. Some folks call him the warrior of the wilderness. Did you know that? That's clever, right? Yeah, so, we first met him some time ago in the north pastures beyond the village and he offered his crew to watch out for us while we were there with the herd. Well, they showed themselves to be trustworthy men, kind, and responsible to Dawit who knows a heap about sheep. So, we gladly accepted and invited them to join us. We had good times hanging out and becoming friends, but mostly they did what they said they would do: protect us and the flocks from the common thieves and raids of desert robbers. They never took anything from us. Having them here meant nothing was able to bother us, whether day or night, whether beast or man. No, sir. No thief was able to plunder us, though one truly scary night, a gang of bandits tried. They attacked without warning from the west and started snatching our sheep and running. Dawit's men went after them and slaughtered each one and I was like—"

"Ibo. Ibo!" My mind is reeling for him to finish. "Please get to the point."

"Yes, yes. Ten of Dawit's men came into camp not long ago. We greeted them and escorted them to Massa who they saluted most respectfully in Dawit's name and made inquiry, you know, on behalf of Dawit, on what was due them on a day of plenty. Food and drink and the like, you know, for protecting us. It's a wise and righteous thing to request. Sheep farmers do that, you know; give good pay to security guards, you know? We have more than enough to share, and they deserve it. Well, Massa flat out refused."

"And, in the cruelest way," Mushi takes over. "He spit and cursed at them, asking 'Who is this Dawit?' and 'Why would I give food to Dawit that is set aside for my house?' He acted as if he didn't know who Dawit was, but we know he does."

"Right," Basaka adds. "He even hid the fact that Dawit provided services to him from Melek Shaul. The Kalebite dog that he is. We felt shame and as weaklings. A few of us tried to stop Massa, to change his mind, but he wouldn't hear it. He waved us off, going on to call Dawit and his men misfits, thieves, and workers of Ba'al. He cried out in laughter that Dawit was nothing more than a disobedient slave on the run from his master and that Dawit better be glad that the king was attending to other business else he would call for the king's men to come and collect Dawit's head on a platter."

My jaw drops. *Foolish Nabal. This could get us all killed.*

"How did they react?" Moh asks before I can get it out.

"They did nothing. They said nothing." Ibo's voice is softer, calmer. "They got back on their mules and rode away. We know them and we know that this is not over. They'll be back here soon, maybe even after sundown, and it won't be for good. Not good at all. Our foolish lord has repaid good with evil, you know, and it's sure to bring death to him and all of us in his house. His wickedness is falling on our heads." We stare at one another as Ibo's words hang in the air.

"It has," Moh breaks the silence.

"We came straight here to you, Aby, because we trust you to know what to do." Basaka is nearly rubbing his chocolate knuckles white while Mushi rocks back and forth with his arms crossed in front of him.

"But, in a way," Moh ignores Basaka's plea for salvation. "It's good news for you, Aby, and possibly us. Dawit is sure to kill Nabal and his chiefs, which means you'll be free. We all might be free. Yahu has answered you."

I close my eyes, stilling myself. *My vision at Bet Tsur: Dah, standing in a fiery tree.* "I don't think so."

"How could it not be?" Moh slants his head probingly. "Nabal's ways have finally caught up with him."

"That may be true," I ponder. "No doubt, Dah is furious by now and will act quickly. But this is not a good situation for the man who would become the next Ebre king . . . an honorable king . . . a blameless king. Deadly retaliation in this way and within our nation and for a fool is not Yahu's doing. I cannot let it happen. Nor will I risk death upon so many here, by intent or accidentally, just so the evil that is Nabal no longer exists to torment me."

"What are you going to do, then?" Ibo asks with his eyes lit up in eager expectation of a reasonable solution. *Good question. Yahu, guide my mind, make our path clear, and till your son's heart to shed anger.*

"Do you know where Dawit and his men are camped?" I ask Ibo.

"They are in the wild forest, almost twenty miles southeast of here where the cliffs are white and sharp, and the thickets are, well, thick."

"Overlooking the sea." Moh simplifies. "Masud."

"Then his route to Karmil will likely be up from the valley of Yashar," I say with nods of agreement from everyone. "Between the two hills. That's our best chance to engage him before he gets here, if not for Nabal, then surely for the innocent others. And for Dah. Here's the plan and tell no one else. No one. And may Yahu guide and protect us."

CHAPTER 22

BESTIR

[bih-stur]: to rouse.

IBO, MUSHI, AND BASAKA GO OVER to the animal stalls to make ready six donkeys and a wagon then wait behind the row of tents closest to the right side of the food house. Moh, Pai, Ahi, and I are already there, quickly collecting a traveling feast of every food we can find. Five dressed sheep and two slabs of dried goat. Two hundred loaves of barley bread and thirty crocks of lentil stew. Five quarts of roasted grain and nuts. Four pots of roasted gourd and garlic. Two hundred fig cakes. One hundred clusters of raisins. Fifty jugs of date preserves, sixty of pickled cucumbers, thirty of leeks and black radishes, and fifteen of honey. Two skins each of water, goats' milk, beer, wine, and new pomegranate juice. "For a private meeting," Moh answers anyone who asks. *I hope it will be enough.*

With the loads secure, the six of them head out the front gate. I run to my tent, change into my lightweight white and gold tunic, spruce up my face, hair, and lips, hook on my wedding ear and nose rings, and cover my head with my short veil. I grab my bag of yellow ribbons and stuff it into the long veil from my tent.

Uzi and I take the same route as the others, left outside the main gate and down over the rocky terrain of Karmil's hill. The strong summer sun shines a spotlight on a distant mountain range. Another rider, followed closely by a swarm of others that together create a dusty ground cloud, descends the majestic hill opposite me. Dawit, I imagine.

I bestir Uzi to go faster, and we do, reaching the flat valley before the advancing squadron comes into view though the ground quivers at the pounding of their coming. *Hallel Yahu*. Moh and the others wait in the middle of the valley. I stop a bit in front of them, hop off Uzi, and spread the long veil on the ground. Rocks wrapped with long yellow ribbons steady its four corners. Then, I kneel face down to the ground in the middle of the veil and wait.

Bitterness and anger compelled me to act compulsively, dishonoring Abbah and ignoring the arranged marriage tradition of my Eber culture. It made me wife to a fool and co-wife with a demon. Had I not, my inner eyes and ears would have remained closed to Yahu's invite for me to be a wise woman. My path would not have crossed with my kindred companions, Uzi, Moh, and Ahi. I would have missed out on the kindness of Pai, Bentah, Ibo, and others. Ifrah, Lami-Yaj, Nimtsa, and Seth would not be family and the first family of a new, holy sanctuary for thrown-away children to heal and thrive. And I would not be here at this place at this time to save my heart's love.

The swirl of the yellow ribbons, the shaking of the earth, the raging dust, and the clanking of iron and bronze swords, daggers, and spears all slow as Dah's band draws closer and finally stops ahead of me. The lone member walks up to my head. Familiar feet in typical male sandals.

A shadow indicates a short tunic with tassels all around the hem.

"Forgive your servant, my Ash, for hindering your duty. May I speak?"

"Abyga'el?" Confusion covers his question. "Is . . . is it you?"

"May I speak, my lord?"

"Yellow ribbons. You're the child rescuer?"

"It is I who needs rescuing." I bestir Yahu to strengthen my heart. "Please, my lord, may I speak?"

"Yes, yes, please do." His agitation is apparent as he offers me his hand. "Get up and tell me what's going on. Since I see no discarded children, why are you here?"

I take his hand, rising slowly. "You are mostly right, my lord. There are no children right here, but there is an ornery and reckless child in Karmil rudely throwing insults and committing theft—one who is so ill-imagined in his spirit that he constantly beckons his own physical demise which, in this instance, is imminent by my lord's own hand."

"It is unwise and dangerous for the imprudence of children to go unnoticed."

"That is true, my lord. Yet, a foolish child, especially one so aptly named by his father and mother, will speak and act vainly without pondering the consequences of his actions on himself or innocent others. That is sheer folly which must be dealt with in exceptionally profound ways."

"Which I intend to do this day."

"Yes, I understand, which is why I am here. Such an ill-natured child requires sound supervision to alleviate evil outcomes."

"And how does this concern you? Has this child tacked a yellow ribbon to a tree?"

"In a sense. By my own hand, I am bound by an arrangement to . . . to the child."

"An arrangement?" Dawit asks with baffling eyes scrutinizing mine now filling up with tears. "No, no, no. You are not his wife. You can't be."

"I am that in name and on paper only. No more than that. Please trust my words."

"How? When?" He looks skyward with his hands clasped on his head as if to keep it from exploding and spilling everywhere. "You cannot imagine the desires and dreams I've had of and for you, Aby, since that first day in Gan Aby some three earth revolutions ago."

"But I can. I have had them of you too." My body, warm from inside as well as out, yearns to merge with his now but my heart and mind elect wisdom.

"May Yahu purge me for such thoughts of a married woman."

"I am not married in the way that you think, but even that doesn't matter right now. What does matter is what happens today. I should have watched over the words and actions of the child more closely. I did not see the righteous men who came to Karmil on your behalf. Had I done so, then I would have made sure that he granted your due petition. But I am here now, Dah, my Ash, with petitions of my own." His face and body relax, allowing room for my continuing intrusion.

"I first ask that you direct your wrath at me and not the child. Killing him would be much like taking the fringe of the king's garment. Find mercy to forgive me for my failure to manage the child. Don't do it for him; do it for you, a man after Yahu's own heart. Secondly, I beg you to accept my gift of food and drink for the men who serve you. Let them refresh their tongues and satisfy their bellies." I point to the great load of gifts and continue my plea.

"Lastly, I entreat Yahu to bestir you now to refrain from enacting vengeance on your enemy. Instead, let Yahu deal with the foolish child and his royal playmate who seeks to take your life, tossing them away like small pebbles from a sling, so that my lord does nothing evil of his own hand. So that no wrongdoing is found in you as long as you live. So that my lord stays clean of taking innocent blood, only fighting the battles ordered by Yahu. So that my Ash will regret nothing when the time of your rising as king is full and Yahu deals well with you, making for you an enduring house, as promised—a blessing not obtained by war or power or might, but only through righteousness, and shifting from what's physical to the spiritual, and good. Choose good, my Ash, and when Yahu does this, please remember me."

Dah steps closer and lowers to his knees, taking my breath away again. *Why is he kneeling before me?* He takes a long, deep breath before he looks up and speaks.

"Yahu has delivered me, once more, and kept me whole and righteous with atonement. Evil does not separate us. I praise Yahu for sending you, my Ayish, as my shield, stopping me from taking the blood guilt of Nabal and all his men as I swore and was on my way to do. I give you gratitude, my heart, for your wisdom and spirit and bravery to even dare stand in my way."

He grasps my hands and rises slowly, his sling and kidskin bag skim my legs, my thighs, my abdomen, my breasts as his deep eyes and warm breath lead the way. That familiar heat wave, now ten times hotter, rushes down my spine, between my legs, and back up to my throat. "Of the vast beauty in all Eber Y'israel, you are the most magnificent; even more today than when we communed in Ramah. I want to . . ." *And I want him to.* He pauses. "I see you and me . . ." He shakes his head to disturb his thoughts. "No, I will not. But what I will do is accept the salvation of Yahu from your lips and of your hands. All is well. Take this as a sign of my word," he whispers as he takes off the gold necklace from around his neck and places it on mine. Its crescent-shaped, onyx, and gold amulet falls to my breast.

"Go, stay strong at heart, and be at peace," Dah continues. "Now, I know where you are, and you will see me again soon . . . one way or another."

He mounts his beast, his men unload the wagon, and they ride back to their majestic hill. We watch until their dust settles then start our return to Karmil.

"Massa won't believe or like this news," Ibo states the obvious.

"He'll be too drunk to hear it," Basaka also states the obvious.

"When he does, I bet he will pee his loincloth," Pai seldom shares her thoughts and certainly not within a group.

"That joy will be all mine," I say. We all laugh into the dimming twilight.

CHAPTER 23

BEMUSED

[bey-muzed]: marked by confusion.

WHEN WE GET BACK, MASSA IS dancing around the firepit near the stage on the central court with half-naked women, spilling the drink out of his goblet, and singing loudly in a slurred voice. His guardsmen try to coax him into a cushion to sit, but he pops right back up, dancing and singing. It's a crazy loop that doesn't appear to be ending anytime soon. This scene is old and so is the night. My news will have to keep until tomorrow when Nabal's veins no longer hold wine. The group parts ways, each tending to work or animals or an evening meal or tents or sleep.

The long veil is back up as the curtain to my tent. I lie on my bed cushions, yawning to stay awake to recount the day. My Ash. His body. The amulet. The second such gold-chained amulet given to me by men I love. Dah received this one from Shaul in more favorable times, I now remember Dah telling me, when he handed out gifts to his sons during a Sukkot feast. I finger it and its inscription. The name, "Yahushua." *Yahu is salvation.* It's a peace that lulls me to sleep.

I wake up singing a tune Emah taught me many moons ago.

Happy just to be.
Happy to be me.
Happy to live free.
Overly, overly, overly, overly.

Happy for anew.
Happy to be true.
Happy to live as one with Yahu.
Overly, overly, overly, overly.

It fits the sparkle of scattered sunlight that greets my step into it, so I continue humming the song in the quiet dawn. Only servants, I think, are stirring.

"Good day to you," I smile at a woman picking up trash and a man repairing a tent, two of only a few people moving around. I sense why. The compound wreaks with the odor of sweaty acid-laden clothes, day-old vomit, and copulation emissions—offerings from the hundreds of people scattered around the grounds snoring, slobbering, and flatulating in their stupor. A hot, though lovely, mid-morning breeze doesn't help at all. I don't see anyone or anything that suggests that Massa is one of them, so I make haste the long way around the central court to get to the main house.

On the porch, cooks are stirring what smells like Noah stew, a dish of cabbage, onion, garlic, turmeric, tarragon, grapeseed oil, lemon, sweet figs, and bitter almonds simmered in coconut and poppy seed milk. It supposedly tames the after-ills of too much strong drink, I guess when the necklace of leaves is of no use. I fill a bowl, place it on a serving tray, and walk with it to the front door, guarded by thugs.

"I am here with remedy for Mas—uh, my lord, Nabal."

"Wait here." He goes inside and returns with a second goon.

"I'll take that," he grumbles and reaches for the tray. "The lord is unavailable."

"I have news that he will want to hear."

"What is it?"

"It's best that I deliver it personally, you know, wife to husband."

"Well, like I said, he is unavail—"

"Is that my little lost lamb, Abyga'el?" Massa yells. "Come, come my dear lamb."

I brush past the goon into the entry room where Massa is reclining on thick cushions, likely too hungover to make it to his bed last night. Surprisingly alert, he eyes me up and down, grinning. I give him much to look at, having decided to wear a long flowy robe in a brilliant blue, orange, and gold stripe that matches the summer sky. Yellow and gold ribbons weave through my braided hair that cascades down my back. A little olive oil on my brown lips gives them a plump sheen.

"I thought you were dead," he starts. "Until I saw you in Ramah. Of course, that was not the time nor the occasion for me to reengage with you in the marital sense."

"I was dead. Dead by your hands and that of your first wife, but now I live."

"No, no, no. I would never harm a curly hair on your head even though you spent many moons away from my house. Where you were and what you were doing, I don't know. As such, you failed to come to my bed when I called you. And now, you enter my humble feast without saying a word to your husband. How does that work, huh, sweetie? Surely, the daughter of the high priest knows better."

"Well of course, she does." I play his tongue-dripping-with-honey game, moving closer to his face. "The high priest and his wife made sure of it. She also knows a mighty warrior when she sees one. And she knows what happens when such a warrior is driven to wrath."

"And what might that be?"

"He attacks, like a roaring and hungry lion. You almost saw it."

"Really? When?"

"Yesterday at twilight, while you were filling yourself with sweet pomegranate wine."

"Yeah?" My heart rate increases with every stretch of his irritating grin.

"Yeah. You see, consistent with the way you tried to manipulate my father, an honorable man, you cheated another beloved Ebre Y'israelite son who simply asked for what was due to him and his men for providing protection for your flocks."

"Aww, hell. I thought you meant something." Nabal waves me off with a chuckle, though his grin starts to fade. "Dirty hoodlums without a home who run around in the desert wilderness? They're nobody. Merely beasts."

"You think so? You owed those hoodlums for many moons of security services across your huge pastures. He believed you would do right by them, especially during your time of harvest. So, they came, his men, asking for a fair payment of food and drink of which you have more than enough to share. But you foolishly refused. 'Who is Dawit?' you asked. A rebellious servant, you called him. You announced that he and his men would get nothing from you."

"And that's what they got," he says arrogantly. "Nothing. Was I supposed to take my bread, my meat, and my wine, and give it to that dog and his fleas? I am the master here. All that you see is mine to do with as I please!"

"So, you thought yourself quite high, having so rudely snubbed him. And you assumed the lion of Y'hudah would accept such disrespect? What your insult did was invite the fury of a kingly army down on your head."

"What do you mean?" He sits up straight.

"Dahwit was on his way here with a sworn oath to Yahu and six hundred men by his side armed with axes, daggers, spears, swords, slings, stones, and bows, to wipe out you and every male belonging to you by this very morning. Would he have done it? Of course, he would have. He is the bear killer. The lion killer. The giant slayer. Shaul killed his thousands? Dawit, tens of thousands."

Nabal stares at me, eyes scowling and forehead veins bulging, bemused by my report.

"As soon as I heard of your evil-doing, I rushed to intercept him and his men in the Yashar valley. Down on my knees, I begged him to turn back his anger and not behave as a fool, like you."

"You're a liar!" Massa yells and spits.

"This is witness to the truth I'm telling you," I hold up the amulet to Massa's face, bemusing him more. Troughs cover his brow. He grips his chest. His eyes widen then roll back into his head and he falls backward onto the cushion like a discarded doll. "Nabal?" I scream. He does not move. Others flood the room and crowd around him, pushing me back toward the door. I leave the house, preferring to sit vigil for him away from the main house.

Massa lies ailing in his bed. I'm told that he opens his eyes for a moment here and there, gazing at the ceiling but does not speak or move his body. Zahra is at the main house almost every hour with her servants, policing the few people allowed to come and go. The goons. Healers. Groomers. A priest. Moh. Maybe Pai. One or two of the royal court, though the king himself is yet to arrive. A few festival guests sing prayers and light candles, but most keep up the self-indulgences they've enjoyed thus far over the next four days when the wool harvest at Har Mihamon officially ends.

Six days later, Massa died in the fleeing dark of night, just before the cock crowed this morning. No one knows the cause of his death. My guess is that his personal crop finally came up from all the deadly seeds he sowed so consistently.

His funeral started a few minutes ago. The full-fledged processional—black-attired wailers, musicians, dancers, and Zahra elegantly dressed in a white betrothal gown with an attendant leading her donkey—traveled about a mile west of the main house to a large, mound-shaped, natural beauty of a basalt outcrop. Nabal called it his heavenly throne on earth.

The service already embodies the harshness and foolishness that was him. His body, lying on a large, gold-colored, walled pad, is covered in a bright, beige, festive robe trimmed in thick, shiny gold and silver stitching. A gold medallion encrusted with twelve jeweled ravens rests on his chest. Gold rings and bangles decorate his hands which meet over his stomach and feature long fingernails glazed with gold and silver dust. Surrounding the body is a growing river of grave goods for Massa's afterlife journey: an assortment of his favorite food, spices, and wines; plates, platters, and goblets; drums, lyres, and other instruments; a quiver full of arrows and a sling full of stones, though he did not shoot or sling; a scribal bag, though he did not scribe; and many gameboards, smoking pipes, and lovemaking toys.

Twelve men carry the entire pad to a wooden platform, about four feet tall, built at the height of the outcrop. Beneath it, piles of wood planks. Large stones encircle the structure, protecting the woodpile and, I imagine, Massa's mourners. Priests stand on either side of the structure.

Massa's friends, no doubt full of wine, start to speak from a podium on the ground in front of the platform. They tell stories of their adventures and deeds with Massa, laughing, whooping, hollering, and finally concluding the talk by pouring on the ground a goblet full of wine in the name of Nabal and throwing the goblet into the nearby firepit. Servants pitch an assortment of oil-rubbed meats over the stones and under the platform, lubricating the wood pile. Sheep. Lamb. Goat. Cow. Dog. Horse. Hen. I gag at the sight and smell and sheer waste of food that could feed hungry people.

Even amid this gaudy spectacle, gratitude swells within me like warm leavened bread for countless wonders, though right now, two vibrate the loudest. My now marital status of widow frees me to return to Ramah or Bet Tsur, which I'll do soon and, hopefully, with my friends. Then there's Dawit, leaving the matter of vengeance to Yahu thus leaving his hands clean.

That gratitude suddenly turns to disgust when I see two of Massa's thugs helping the heavily pregnant Zahra stand. With her eyes closed, she moans and sobs and rocks and sways, as if she's intoxicated or in a trance. "I'mmmm commming, meeee lubbbbb. Commmming, lubbbbb." The

thugs usher her up the outcrop and to the wooden platform. They pick her up and lay her gently next to her lord.
She embraces Massa's body as her wails increase, unaware
that the thugs are tying her to the sordid display.

"No!" I stand to declare my protest. She is an evil person, yes, but is not deserving of this horror. "What is this?
What are you doing? Stop this!"

More of the thugs come toward me and Ahi grabs my
arm, shaking her head. Apparently, it's an ancient ritual of
Nabal's maternal family to bury the first wife, if still alive,
with the corpse. It could simply be that Har Mihamon and
Kalebtu have had enough of them both and this impromptu
occasion is expedient. Either way, I refuse to be a part of this
barbarity at best and murder at worst, so I turn around to
leave. Ahi and Pai come behind me. Before we can take ten
steps, the meat-slathered wood underneath the platform
bursts into flames, startling our departure and triggering a
chorus of shrieks, screams, and cheers. A plume of smoke
fills the air.

The deed is done. The monsters are gone. We are still
here and slowly walk back to the compound as friends and
sisters. Moh catches up to us and seems to enjoy the quiet
company.

We arrive at an empty estate. No doubt, another merry
feast will soon erupt from the outcrop of Har Mihamon all
the way to Kalebtu. Before we reach the operations house,
four men ride through the main gate and into the central
courtyard. They stop when our paths cross.

CHAPTER 24

BE WAIFS

[weyf]: outlawry; something found.

"OZEM?"

"Peace, my sister."

"What are you doing here?"

"Looking for you."

"Why? Do you need more food? Did something happen to Dah?"

"No, none of that," he chuckles, gets down off his mule, and hugs me. "We come in peace and on behalf of Dawit. He sent us here to find you and deliver this to you." He hands me a piece of ripped paper. "He wrote it three days ago."

I read it silently and with hope.

My Ayish, my heart is perfectly captivated by
your essence.
Like bees drawn to nectar. Like fish to water.
Like the moon to the sun.

You, whose enthralling beauty is beyond
compare.
With a complexion of the sun-kissed anise
fruit.
Lips of the sweet rose plum.
Locs of a thousand black lambs, and
The alluring body of curly maple wood.
And that is only the exterior,
The skin on the grape, protecting what's in-
side.
What captivates me is your flawless heart
Which is richer than garments woven with
gold and
Warmer than a mother's breast, fragrant truth
that seduces me.

Me, who roams throughout Kanaan just to
stay alive,
Not knowing where I will land.
Me, who wants you for my own.
But what shall I give for one such as yourself?
What should I render for your hand?
I have nothing to pay besides myself.
All I have is my heart that will forever love
you.
My strength to protect you, and
My word to provide for you.
That is all I have, and I freely offer it to you.
If you will, come to me and be my betrothed.
And let us create a new garden together,
One that flourishes as the blessings of
Abrah'm.

"What does it say?" Pai clasps her hands to her chest.

"We are to bring you to him to be his wife," O says. "If it so pleases you." Ahi hops up and down as the others express their *oohs* and *aahs*.

"It does," I answer, tears streaming on the outside and gratitude rising again on the inside. "My hope of us was lost but now it is waif, and I will be most pleased to go to my beloved." A deep inhale and exhale calm my excitement and give me a moment of composure to inquire to O, "I will not be going alone. Is that acceptable?"

"It is my sister. Whatever you need."

"We are all going." I turn to my friends. "We are family, and family stays together."

"Count me in," Ahi is quick to respond. "I get enlivening vibrations from that Dawit and his crew."

"A part of me will always be with you, Aby," Pai says. "But my heart belongs here. With Ibo."

"What?" Ahi and I both gasp at her revelation. "That's amazing. We didn't know. How exciting." We go on and on.

"That leaves the three of us, then," I say, embracing Moh and Ahi.

Moh shakes and hangs his head. "I, too, cannot go."

"That's ridiculous," I chide. "Of course, you can. I would not go without you."

"The business here and in Kalebtu are—"

"And all of it—the land and the livestock—belongs to Ahi, Pai, and me now. And most likely to my new husband." I take his hands. "Look, Moh, sheepshearing is over. Ibo can handle things here. Mushi and Basaka can manage Kalebtu, at least for a little while. We can go—me, you, andAhi—connect with Dah and devise a plan with him. Then, return shortly to revive both villages into what we truly want them to be. What do you think?"

"I think you excluded Uzi," Moh concedes. "Don't forget him."

"Never. Let's get our stuff. And, Ahi, leave the skin salve behind. It is not needed in the wilderness."

After a few hours, I mount Uzi and, with my cohorts beside me, go with Dah's men to become his wife. My delight is in not looking back. I came to the wilderness of Ma'on betrothed to a fool and now I leave it betrothed to the wise warrior my heart longed for. My Ash, with whom I rejoice to roam the forests of Kanaan and be waifs— outlaws in our land.

Acknowledgments

I simply and happily thank these special few of many beautiful elements in my universe:

My life partner, W. J., my very own Dawit, whose passionate belief and enduring encouragement (with a dash or two of tough love) propel me forward to the finish line.

My children, Jay and Biruk, the suns of my double-star solar system, and William, the bonus moon I didn't know would be in my sky, for helping light the way along my darkest writing days.

My sisterlike and canny sounding board, Vikki, who is ever ready to conspire on my behalf.

My first-responder readers, Katrina "Wink" and Rosie, for being brave enough to wade through and place prudent eyes upon crappy first drafts.

The publishing team at BookLogix, who went to the moon and back to coddle and dress this book for its market debut.

My brothers, Terry and Al, sisters-in-love, and their families for being fundamental constants around me and any wild-hair adventures I may undertake.

My other kindred friends (you know who you are) and Cuzzos (you know, Roberta's daughters) who always summon the best in me.

A Most Useful Betrothal is here, and in a far better state, because of you all.

About the Author

Netta Fei is a practicing writer enchanted with the divine feminine energy exhibited by bold women. Growing up a preacher's kid at a southern US Black Baptist church, she developed a healthy (yet taboo) questioning of biblical and other ancient texts which inform her stories today. Netta is the recipient of the Georgia Writers' 2023 John Lewis Grant for Fiction. Visit www.nettafei.com to learn more.

Printed in the USA
CPSIA information can be obtained
at www.ICGtesting.com
LVHW092144221024
794573LV00004B/25

9 798990 138117